RISKY WITCHNESS

HAUNTED HAVEN
BOOK TWO

ADA BELL

RISKY WITCHNESS

Enjoy this enchanting second installment in the Haunted Haven series by award-winning author Ada Bell!

After her early days in Willow Falls nearly got her killed, Emma treats herself to a nice, peaceful day at a spa with her ghostly grandfather. With free coffee, fluffy bathrobes, and luxurious linens, this place is heaven for a thread witch. Or it would be, if not for that guy who won't get off his cell phone. Darren is so rude, loud, and condescending, Emma is barely surprised when she finds him dead on the massage table. Unfortunately, after news of their disagreement spread, she quickly becomes the prime suspect.

Darren was a high-powered businessman. He didn't care who got hurt on his way to the top. Investigating his death means following a trail of wronged business associates, hoodwinked partners, estranged relatives, and wrongfully fired employees. The more Emma digs, the more suspects she finds. To make matters worse, the local police officers have noticed her talking to people who aren't there. Suddenly, helping Darren becomes a risky proposition. Can Emma find the real killer before she gets locked up?

PRAISE FOR ADA BELL

"*Mystic Pieces* is a charming, humorous, and original mystery that weaves a tale of murder and self-discovery with heart, family, and psychic visions."

— READER'S FAVORITE

"...I liked Aly as a main character and reading about her and her powers. I liked the side characters and how each had their own personality that made it easy to remember. All in all I really enjoyed this book and look forward to the next book in the series!"

— LOLA'S BOOK REVIEWS

"A cute and cozy introduction to the quirky and devoted characters, *Mystic Pieces* is the perfect first installment to the Shady Grove Psychic Mystery Series."

— LITERARY LIONESS

Empress Books

P.O. Box 1572

Clifton Park, NY 12019

RISKY WITCHNESS

HAUNTED HAVEN

To Suzanne,

Thank you for bestowing your daughter on this world. Michelle is wonderful.

I see dead people.

— COLE SEAR, *THE SIXTH SENSE*

ONE

My grandfather settled onto the chaise lounge beside mine, stretched out, and made himself comfortable. He'd exchanged his usual tattered-bathrobe look for a fluffy, snow-white robe and gray rubber flip-flops provided by the fancy spa where we were spending the day. Just a normal grandfather-granddaughter outing.

Except Walter Sparrow was dead.

We never knew each other while he was alive, and he'd been alone for almost thirty years since he passed away. After we found each other, I'd promised to take my ghostly grandfather places he never got to go. This fancy spa beat his first suggestion: skydiving. I'd explained that he couldn't use most of the services, but he wanted to come. Even ghosts enjoyed a good hot tub, apparently. Despite not being able to feel the water, the steam, or the jets, he found the whole idea soothing.

This place was incredible. The lobby was nice enough: clean and airy, but nothing special. Barely a hint of what awaited inside. My jaw dropped when I entered the locker room. I'd expected your average gym facilities, not wood-paneling, plush cushions, and a marble counter offering flat irons and hair dryers. The lockers themselves filled a space bigger than my first apartment. Beyond that, a hallway took me past several bathroom stalls, four sinks, a sauna, a water cooler, and more.

Upon leaving the locker room, patrons got to choose between two separate, equally lush waiting areas. On the terrace, spa goers could relax on couches or sit in the hot tub while sipping coffee and listening to light jazz music piped through discreetly placed speakers. I could happily live here forever.

"Ahhhhh," Walter said, closing his eyes. "This is the life. We should do this more often."

"No argument here," I murmured.

"What's that? Speak up!"

Between the locker room and the terrace was the Relaxation Room, where we awaited my next treatment. This calming room held scattered chaise lounges, dim lighting, and sound machines to discourage talking. Stone pillars, a massive fireplace, and scattered candles contributed to the ambiance. A fountain bubbled peacefully in the center of the room. Signs everywhere reminded us that this was a silent area.

Instead of answering Walter, I grinned before shooting a look at the "No Talking" sign on the wall beside him.

"Pfft. That's for humans," he said. "What can they do, toss me out? I'd like to see them try."

Smiling at the mental image his words invoked, I leaned back and closed my eyes. No people, no noise, just the gentle roar of the sound machine and the fountain's soothing babble. Idly, my fingers traced a pattern on the thick cushion, reveling in the tactile feel beneath my palm. In response, it purred, a cheerful hum only I could hear.

Walter was right: this life rocked.

A cry of outrage made my eyes fly open. To my surprise, a dark-haired man sporting silver streaks at the temples had parked himself on the chair beside me, despite the several other available chairs. Although sitting, he appeared to be about medium height and stocky. His demeanor reminded me of Tony Soprano. Arrogance oozed out of every pore, even with his back to me.

Poor Walter wriggled indignantly beneath the interloper.

"Excuse me," I whispered, wanting to respect the room's rules but also get him to move. "My grandfather was sitting there."

"They can't get cold feet," the man said. "We've got a contract. I don't care if someone offered a lower rate: they've already signed. That's our account. We're doing the work; they're paying us. Period. They don't have to use the ideas."

"What?" I understood each of his words, but not together in response to my statement.

Too late, I realized he wore a Bluetooth earpiece. Apparently, the rules didn't apply to big shots. My phone was in the locker room where it belonged, as his should be. I tapped his shoulder and pointed to the sign, but he shrugged me off. "Then I'll see you in court."

How rude.

"Some people!" Walter slithered out from underneath the usurper and put his hands on his hips. "Aren't you going to say something?"

"I tried!" I kept my voice as low as possible, even though my new neighbor was engrossed in his obnoxiously loud conversation.

Walter and I chose this section of the room because it was private. A bunch of plants isolated us from the other spa-goers. All I could see were the rude guy and his teacup —which inexplicably sat on my side of the small table between our chairs. For a long moment, I contemplated accidentally spilling it on his head. Instead, I pushed it back where it belonged.

Pulling myself to my feet, I went to find an attendant. Someone needed to tell him to be quiet or, better yet, go away. The next room contained a hot tub, a tea and coffee station, and several couches but no employees. Finally, back in the locker room, I found a girl who appeared to be in her twenties with short, spiky blond hair and the easily identifiable spa employee uniform. She wore bright eye makeup and a broad smile. Her name tag identified her as Missy.

"Excuse me," I said. "I'm sorry to bother you, but there's a man shouting into his cell phone in the Relaxation Room."

She closed her eyes and shook her head slightly. "I'm sorry. It must be Darren."

"You know him?"

"Everyone around here knows Darren. Unfortunately," she said. "He comes in twice a week to get a massage. Always demands Eve, won't let anyone else do it. Stays in the room for ages. But he's a regular, and he tips well, so he pretty much gets to do what he wants."

"I'll give you twenty dollars to tell him to be quiet. I tried, but he ignored me."

She snorted. "I said he tips *well*. Sorry. Mrs. Bracken wants to keep him happy. But listen, it's after nine-thirty. He should go in soon. Usually, he showers and leaves when he's done, so you won't see him again. Enjoy your stay and try not to think about him."

That was a relief. I thanked Missy and headed back into the lounge area. Since my appointment wasn't for another fifteen minutes, I poured myself a cup of tea. Maybe if I took long enough, my spot would be empty when I returned.

No such luck. Although I dawdled, Mr. Bigshot—Darren —was still there. Now he lay sprawled across the lounger, eyes closed, but still speaking loudly into the phone. His legs reached uncomfortably close to where I'd been sitting. My grandfather had moved into my old chair, leaving me with no choice but to perch awkwardly at the end and pretend this was how I relaxed. I refused to move when he invaded my space. But I also didn't want to upset Walter more by lying on top of him.

After I settled, Walter asked, "Did you give 'em the what for? Curse his wrinkly bits?"

With a glance to confirm Mr. Bigshot wasn't paying any attention to me, I whispered, "I wish. Apparently, he's very important and has a lot of money. People around here let him do whatever he wants."

"That's why you should curse him. He'll never see it coming."

"I thought witches were supposed to use our powers for good."

"There's some debate about what 'for good' really means," Walter replied. "For example, if you made his robe sew itself around his legs and knock him over, would that hurt anyone?"

"Probably Mr. Bigshot," I said, smothering a laugh. Although I possessed a fair dose of hearth magic, my expertise lay in ambient thread magic. Regular magic came from spells, but ambient magic involved drawing power from the world around me.

Hearth and home spells could be hit or miss while I worked on growing my powers, but thread usually did what I wanted. Some types more than others. It was entirely possible that I could pull off Walter's suggestion. But unlike my grandfather, I didn't see 'for good' as open to interpretation.

This was supposed to be a relaxing grandfather-granddaughter excursion. It might be fun to fantasize about turning this jerk's clothes on him, but the idea made me tense. The aftermath wouldn't be soothing.

A spa attendant approached. She was very pretty, with warm brown eyes behind burgundy glasses that really popped. Her long, dark hair was pulled back into a low bun. She smiled softly at the man beside me. "Mr. Cartwright?"

To my surprise, he put his phone away before responding. "Eve! Nice to see you. How are you?"

She blushed. *Blushed?* "If you're ready, it's time for your service."

"Almost." He stood up, then turned to the teacup on the table between our lounge chairs. He tossed the whole thing back in one gulp, then grimaced and shook his head. "Who made this batch? It's too bitter. Someone let it steep too long."

"I'm very sorry," Eve said. "I'll ask Mrs. Bracken to have someone make a new pot immediately."

"Let's just go."

As Mr. Bigshot exited, most of the tension left my

shoulders. I gestured at the now-empty chair beside me. "Do you mind moving back?"

"Why don't you move?" Walter asked.

"Because it's weird for me to jump into his chair the second he leaves. No one would see you do it."

He grumbled, but switched. When I leaned back and settled down to regain my serenity, my grandfather was still talking to himself. I opened one eye. "Don't let Mr. Bigshot ruin your day. We're here to have fun."

"Yeah, yeah," he said. "You're right. I love this stuff. Even if I can't fully appreciate it."

"Me, too."

Someone else walked by, so Walter slumped back against his seat and closed his eyes. He was sad that he couldn't get a massage. He'd wanted me to book an extra room and leave it empty, but I refused. The people of Willow Falls already thought I was strange. Walter had every intention of joining me in the hot tub, though. He'd been dead a long time, so I let it go. As long as he avoided the locker room, he was free to explore.

"Emma Faden?"

At the sound of my name, I opened my eyes. Missy stood a few feet away, wearing a serene smile. "Hello, again. I'll be doing your body wrap today. Would you like anything to drink before we begin?"

I started to say, no, I had tea when Mr. Bigshot's parting words echoed in my mind. Too bitter, he'd said. My lips pursed at the thought. "Some water, please."

"I'd be happy to. Right this way." She led me down a winding hall, past several closed doors with floral paintings hanging between them. Thick carpeting absorbed our foot-steps. Dim lighting and low music contributed to the overall ambiance. They'd done a great job creating a place where you could forget the outside world existed. Until someone came in, flopped down next to you, and started shouting into a cell phone.

No. That wasn't helpful.

When we entered the room, I put Mr. Bigshot out of my mind, hopefully forever.

TWO

Missy showed me into a small, cozy room dominated by a rectangular table draped with fluffy white towels. They looked almost as plush and cozy as my robe. My magic told me they were made of similar cloth. There was a fireplace on the far wall, although this one wasn't lit. A small fountain on the mantel filled the room with soothing sounds. Softly piped-in music from the corners of the ceiling would lull me to sleep once the service began. Vases filled with white flowers stood in each corner. Everything was clean, soft, and serene. The scent of lavender filled the air, relaxing me even further.

Then a metal drain in the tile floor caught my attention. Above the bed, there was this massive metal thing that looked like some kind of torture device. The bottom looked similar to an IV rack: a tall metal pole attached to a stand on wheels. The top was a long bar with several half circles hanging off it, along with a bunch of knobs. All together, it resembled something a person might use if trying to get information from an uncooperative suspect.

"What on earth is that?" I asked.

She laughed. "That's for after you're unwrapped. To rinse all the scrub off without you having to stand up. I'll wash your hair and everything. It's incredibly relaxing."

That also explained the drain. The entire room doubled as a giant shower.

This was only my second body wrap ever. The first happened twenty years ago, when a friend insisted on a spa day instead of a traditional bachelorette party. It had taken me six months to pay off the credit card charges. But the service itself evoked happy memories, and I was excited for the experience, creepy, horror-movie shower thingy and all.

Coming here had been a great idea, even though Walter couldn't benefit from the full range of services. Maybe I could take notes and set up a spa for ghosts back at the mansion. It would never work, obviously, but the idea high-lighted how much my life had changed in the past few months.

"Well, well, well. This is pretty cushy, ain't it?" Walter said as he fluttered around the room. I'd gotten used to him talking to me when there were other people in the room, and he mostly accepted that I couldn't respond directly.

"Beautiful fireplace," I said to Missy.

Walter grinned at me before settling onto the table and wiggling his hips. "Oh, I bet this is soft. A man could get used to this."

Missy asked a few questions about my medical history and goals for the session, while I tried to ignore the happy moans emanating from the surface behind her. When she finished, she asked, "Do you have any questions?"

Yeah, how did I lie on the table comfortably when a ghost took up the entire surface? I'd have to bribe him into getting up once she left the room. I drained my cup, then held it up to get a moment alone with my grandfather. "Can I have more water, please?"

"Certainly. I'll get it while you change." She showed me a hook on the door. "Hang your clothes there. Take off your robe, jewelry, and anything else you're comfortable with. Leave your shoes by the fireplace and hang your robe on that hook. When you finish, lie facedown on the table and put your face in the cradle. There's a dish on the hearth for small items. I'll be right back."

My fingers went to the locket around my neck as the door closed. I didn't want it to get tangled in my hair, oiled up, or broken during the session. As unlikely as that seemed, considering this necklace originally belonged to Grandma Vera, I preferred to be safe. The heart-shaped locket contained pictures of her and my grandfather when they were young and in love. He gave it to her as a gift; she'd returned it when they'd broken up. Poor guy. He hadn't known she was pregnant.

Although I'd loved the grandfather I knew growing up, Grandma Vera's affair with Willow Falls' most energetic and outgoing resident made me wish they could have stayed together. He would've been fun to play with as a child. Despite my personal history, I was a sucker for a good love story. It made me sad that Vera and Walter never got their happily ever after.

Which was why I was in a massage room with a ghost, getting spa treatments. On the same table, if he wouldn't move.

The reminder jerked me back to the present. I'd been lost in memory for too long. Missy would return any second, and I stood staring into space.

"Wait!" Walter yelled as I lifted my arms around the back of my neck to remove the chain. "Don't take it—"

His words cut off abruptly when the clasp opened, and my grandfather disappeared.

Oops.

"Walter?"

No response.

Oh, no!

I'd forgotten he could only leave the mansion when I wore this necklace. The past few weeks, I kept my locket on most of the time. Both because the magic inside let Walter explore more of the world than his five-thousand-square-foot home and because it kept me connected to both grandparents. I enjoyed spending time with him and hearing stories of Grandma Vera when she was young. But I'd never taken the locket off while away from home, and that apparently broke the spell.

Now Walter's special day had been cut short because of my thoughtlessness. A wave of guilt hit me, even though I hadn't sent him away on purpose. I should have remembered the power of the locket and kept it on.

Hopefully, I'd find him back at the house. We hadn't experimented with what happened if our connection got severed. It would be terrible if he got stuck somewhere.

Stupid. I felt absolutely terrible, but I couldn't do anything to improve the situation. With my phone locked away, I couldn't even call home to ask my friend and cook Josie to pass Walter a message. (Which was iffy, anyway, since she couldn't find him without our magic cat's help.) I'd have to make it up to my grandfather when I got home. We might wind up skydiving, after all.

"Sorry!" I whispered, knowing Walter couldn't hear.

With a sigh, I set the locket in the dish left for that purpose. I slid my weird rubber spa shoes off and left them beside the hearth. My robe went on the hook, then I examined the massage table.

Now that I knew this service ended in a horizontal shower, covering the bed with towels instead of sheets made sense. When I put my hand out to touch them, the towel's threads warmed to my touch. "Hello there. It's nice to meet you, too."

My greeting brought joy to the fabric, and my smile widened. The towels were so soft. One hundred percent Egyptian cotton, with long-staple fibers, which sounded scratchy but caressed the body amazingly. Although I loved most fabrics, I had to admit this was one of my favorites.

Since Missy would be back soon, I couldn't spend all day stroking the table. I pulled the top towel back and climbed onto the table, noting with pleasure that it was warm. Did the threads do that for me?

This witch thing was so cool!

Not a moment too soon, I put my face into the cradle at the top of the table, and the top towel pulled itself up to my shoulders. Ahhh. Perfect.

A knock sounded. I called out to let Missy in.

"Is the table too hot?" she asked as she re-entered.

"Hold on. You know the table is warm?"

She laughed. "Of course. It's a heated table. You thought I left the thermostat blazing on my way out?"

That made more sense than thinking the threads drew heat into themselves purely to make me happy, so I went with it. "It's amazing. My bed at home needs this."

"You and me both." She moved toward me, and her feet came into my field of view. White sneakers, so clean they looked brand new. Her white socks had little rainbow cats on them. Pink, my cat, would have approved. He might even have told her so.

Once Missy began the full-body exfoliation, I closed my eyes and let my mind empty. Things had been busy hectic since my bed-and-breakfast opened, what with my original cook getting murdered and Josie getting accused of killing her. We'd found the actual murderer before it was too late, but still. This service was long overdue. Wrapping myself in towels and doing nothing but relaxing felt like dying and going to heaven.

Missy's ministrations had nearly lulled me to sleep when she asked me to roll over onto my back. A few minutes later, she told me she had finished applying the full-body exfoliating scrub, and it was time to do the wrapping.

"You can leave your hands at your side or cross them over your chest, but decide now. There's no changing positions once you're wrapped."

"What do you recommend?"

"Crossing them can help create more of a cozy feeling— like swaddling an infant. But it's up to you."

After thinking for a minute, I crossed my arms over my chest. She moved around the table, wrapping each towel tightly around me. By the time she'd finished, I couldn't move at all, but I felt safe and warm. Like a caterpillar beginning chrysalis.

Once she finished, she applied a thick face mask that smelled like honey. "I'm going to let you soak in the mask, remove the toxins from your skin. In about twenty minutes, I'll come back to wash your hair and rinse you off."

I nodded before realizing she wouldn't see the movement in the dim light. "Sounds good. Thanks."

A moment later, the door clicked shut. I let the soft music take me back to my happy place. It didn't take much before I moved back into the semi-napping state achieved before Missy wrapped me up.

A shout made my eyes fly open.

What was happening? Did I dream that? Weird dream. I shook my head and tilted my head to one side to listen. It didn't feel like something inside my head. Somewhere, a real person had cried out for help.

The yell came again. The sound was definitely real. Somewhere beyond the left wall, a person was highly distressed.

My first instinct was to stand, but Missy had wrapped me up tight. I could wiggle my toes and blink, but not move much else. Help for that individual would probably arrive before I could get to them. Help, and possibly judgment day.

I couldn't just lie there, though. When the shouting continued, I tried to uncross my arms. Nothing happened. An exasperated sigh escaped me. Missy must have made mummies in a past life.

But Missy wasn't a witch, and her work couldn't keep me down.

With a silent prayer, I asked the towel's threads to let me out. The fabric shot open. The topmost towels draped across my legs and belly flew across the room. I was free!

Swinging my legs around the table, I hopped down. I made it three strides down the hall before realizing my lack of clothing. There was no time to go back for my robe. I asked it to come to me. As soon as the fabric settled around my shoulders and the tie wrapped around my waist, my pace increased.

The hallway was empty. Still, the shouting continued. Not words, just terrified sounds. I tried to determine whether there was more than one person in the room, but it sounded like one voice. No other signs of a problem.

I ran toward the commotion. How many people were in that room? Did someone get locked inside by mistake? Where were the spa employees? Why wasn't anyone helping? The walls here couldn't be soundproof if I'd heard the uproar—did all the other patrons bring noise-canceling earmuffs?

No, because the staff should still hear this person's cries. Their lack of concern gave me pause. Maybe nothing was wrong, and I was completely over-reacting. These could be normal exercise sounds from the on-site gym, or maybe the noise was part of this person's process, a way of ejecting toxins. What did I know?

But my gut told me something was very wrong, even if no one else had noticed yet. I hurried down the hall and around a corner.

About ten feet ahead of me, the hallway ended. The door to the last room on the left stood ajar. The shouting definitely came from inside that room. I barreled toward the noise, not even stopping to wonder if someone was hiding behind the door. It bounced off the wall with a loud thud.

Inside, I skidded to a halt. The room looked the same as mine, except Mr. Bigshot stood in the middle, shouting. For some reason, he was dressed in a full business suit instead of the bathrobe he'd been wearing earlier. Nice suit, but why would he get dressed and come back here? He was so upset, I could barely make out any of his words.

Before I could ask what was going on, he turned to me. "What is the meaning of this? I demand you fix me at once!"

Fix him? And who was this guy to order me around? I'd come in to save him.

But he was clearly distressed, so I gave him the benefit of the doubt. "I'm sorry, I don't understand."

He pointed at the table. "Fix me! I don't know what you did, but you need to undo it. I'm very busy; I don't have time for your nonsense!"

I opened my mouth, about to apologize for not working here. Although really, I should chastise him for disturbing all the patrons. The words died in my throat when I realized what had caused this guy's agitation.

First, I could see right through him. Second, his body still lay on the table.

THREE

At my horrifying discovery, a gurgle escaped my lips. I'd been so focused on finding the source of the noise, I'd barely glanced at the massage table. Now the truth sank in: What I'd heard wasn't a man screaming for help at all, but his ghost, probably distressed at finding himself dead. Something horrible happened during his treatment.

A stocky man of about medium height lay prone, wearing nothing but a white sheet pulled slightly above his waist. He gazed at the ceiling with unseeing eyes. There didn't appear to be a scratch on him.

I raced toward the table without thinking. The fact that a ghost stood beside me suggested CPR would be futile, but I gave it a shot, anyway. Singing *Staying Alive* to myself to match the beat, I pushed on Darren's chest with all my strength. Then I went to perform mouth-to-mouth and stopped. There was some kind of foam on his lips. I didn't dare touch it, but leaning close, it smelled like vomit. People who died of natural causes didn't throw up, did they? Either way, I wasn't putting my mouth on his.

It wouldn't have helped, anyway. This guy was definitely dead. No breath, no heartbeat. I gazed at him sadly for a long moment. This wasn't my first time finding someone who had passed away unexpectedly, but it didn't get any easier.

Where was his masseuse? It seemed odd that she would have left him alone in the room during his service. Did his therapist take a bathroom break? Seemed unlikely. Unless she'd slipped him something to make him fall asleep, I'd expect him to complain about having his time wasted.

Hmmm.

Beside me, the hysterical ghost was still staring at his body, making horrified sounds.

"There, there," I said. Comforting ghosts was not my forte. My first instinct when someone was upset was to assure them everything would work out fine. Here, that would be cruel.

Instead, I asked, "What happened?"

"I seem to have gotten so relaxed, I learned astral projection," he said. "Get me back in my body!"

"I'm sorry, but I can't do that," I said.

"What happened to you?"

"To me?"

He gestured. "Your face is a mess. You look like Hannibal Lecter."

My hands went to my face. I'd forgotten about the full body and face mask Missy applied, which was starting to crystalize. "Spa treatment. Don't worry about it. I'm here to help."

"Great. Put me back. Wash your hands first."

I forced myself to remain calm. "I'm sorry, but it appears that you died. If you could get into your body, you would have managed without me. Can you tell me what happened?"

"If you didn't come to fix me, what are you doing here?" the ghost demanded. He threw his hands up in the air before pointing at the door. "This is my massage room. It's *private*. Get out!"

"With pleasure," I said.

One demanding ghost in my life was enough, thank you very much. Walter was family. Now that we'd gotten used to each other, it was usually nice having him around. But this guy was a total stranger, and I hadn't particularly liked him during his life. Don't get me wrong—I felt bad that he'd died. But I didn't have to stand around and listen to him make impossible demands.

Spinning on my heel, I turned toward the door.

"Wait!" the man shouted. "Can't you help?"

"What makes you think I can put you back in your body?" I asked.

"One, you're the only person who came to see why I was yelling. Two, you're chatting with me, but you say I'm dead. Regular people can't interact with dead people. You must have a special ability."

He had me there. Too bad Walter had boomeranged back to the mansion (I hoped that was where he went). He might have been able to explain the process of dying better than I could.

Then again, the last time my grandfather met another ghost, he insulted her and sent her racing into the afterlife before I could convince her to help me find her killer. Maybe this initial meeting would go more smoothly with just the two of us.

"Okay, that's a fair point," I conceded. "I can see ghosts. You are, I'm sorry to say, a ghost."

"That's impossible. How did I die?"

"I asked you the same question. But regardless of how it happened, the evidence doesn't lie. Your body is on the table, and you are standing beside it."

His face fell. "Are you sure I'm not astral-projecting?"

"I guess you could be. Do you know how to do that?"

"Well, no. But my wife swears it's a thing. Even a stopped clock is right twice a day, you know what I mean?" His wink made my skin crawl.

Immediately, I vowed to get this man into the light as quickly as possible. "I don't know much about projection, but I believe the person's body remains alive during the process. You, sir, have no pulse."

"Why did you stop doing CPR? You could save me!"

"It's too late. If it wasn't, you'd still be inside. I really am sorry. Finding yourself dead must be quite a shock." I looked around the room. Mostly, it looked like mine. No drain on the floor, no creepy shower bar, but otherwise the same. "Where is your massage therapist? Shouldn't she be here?"

"I guess so. I fell asleep. She lets me stay on the table as long as I want."

"How long ago did she leave?"

"Ten minutes, maybe? We weren't looking at a clock."

This guy appeared to be in a stressful business, considering he'd been arguing about a deal in a day spa. Not to mention threatening to sue whoever he'd been talking to. Maybe he'd had a stroke? A heart attack? "Have you been feeling ill? Chest pains? Anything like that?"

"I'm fit as a fiddle!" He banged on his chest. "Although, now that you mention it, I got dizzy in the hall. Probably stood up too fast. Oh, and my lips went numb. It would have gone away."

Were numb lips and dizziness signs of a heart attack? Or did something else cause his death? This whole situation felt wrong. Plus, there was that stuff on his lips. Everything I'd seen on TV suggested that he'd been poisoned.

"You had tea earlier, right?" As the words left my mouth, I clearly saw myself moving his teacup away from my side of the table. Even though I couldn't have known, I wanted to kick myself. If someone slipped a toxin in the tea, my fingerprints were on the murder weapon. "Did you eat or drink after coming in here?"

"In the massage room? Are you kidding me? What kind of question is that?"

Instead of answering, I looked around for clues. The room seemed undisturbed. The visible parts of the body had no marks. He hadn't consumed anything since entering, but not all toxins worked instantly. He could've been poisoned earlier.

"Can you think of anyone who wanted to hurt you?" I asked.

"Who would want me dead?" He threw his shoulders back and spread his arms. "I am a rich, powerful, handsome man. Everyone loves me."

I'd give him two out of four if I were feeling generous.

If someone committed murder in this room, I'd contaminated the crime scene by touching the body to perform chest compressions. I dearly hoped poor Mr. Bigshot merely suffered a heart attack. Either way, I shouldn't be alone with the body when the police arrived.

Hold on. Were the police coming? Had anyone called them? There was no sign of Eve, and no one else had a reason to be in this room. I patted my pockets before remembering the spa rules: no phones.

Everyone but Mr. Bigshot—Darren. Missy had said his

name was Darren. Since the man died, I should use his real name. He'd had his phone when he came in here.

I turned to look for it. He couldn't possibly have taken an electronic device on the table during the massage, right? On a hearth identical to the one in Missy's massage room, I found a shallow dish like the one that held my locket. It was empty. No phone in the rubber shoes left on the floor, either.

Although massage tables weren't known for their comfort, this one looked as soft and luxurious as any bed. Pure white sheets, soft as a marshmallow, with a matching blanket on top. I touched the edge of the table, closed my eyes, and took a deep breath. The scent of lavender hit me, just like in Missy's room. But there was another odor underlying that. I couldn't identify it, other than noting that it seemed chemical. Some kind of cleaner? Or maybe Darren wore too much aftershave.

Trying to ignore the smell, I reached for the fabric with my magic.

What happened here? I asked silently.

"Hello? Are you napping?" Darren's voice jerked me back into the room.

"I'm thinking about everything you told me."

"Why aren't you calling 911?" He peered intently at me. "Hold on. Didn't I see you in the Relaxation Room?"

"Yeah, you sat next to me," I said. "Give me a second."

As near as I could tell, the only thing on the massage table was Darren. The thin sheet covering him should have shown an outline if his phone had been with him. Besides, most massage places wouldn't allow electronics on the table. He must have left the phone somewhere else.

Unless someone broke in, killed Darren, and stole his phone, it must be in the pocket of his robe. His garment wasn't hanging neatly on the door like mine, though. It took a minute before I spotted the luxurious white cotton lying in a heap on the floor.

I sent a silent apology to the cloth, which deserved better.

"What are you doing?" Darren demanded when I lifted the robe off the ground. He pointed at the door. "This is my massage room. It's *private*. Get out!"

"I'm looking for your phone to call the police."

"Oh. Okay, fine. Better hurry."

Behind me, something crashed to the floor. From the direction of the hallway. A feeling of dread descended upon me. No one should be behind me. I spun around, one hand still in the pocket of Darren's robe.

The pretty girl who got Darren for his service earlier now stood in the doorway, her face flushed. A small plastic bottle lay overturned at her feet. She glanced from the body on the massage table to me and back. Once, twice.

Her mouth opened and closed like she'd forgotten how to speak. I couldn't move. Couldn't breathe.

Then she screamed, a blood-curdling cry.

"Darren! Murderer! Help! She killed Darren!"

CHAPTER

FOUR

Darren rushed past me to put his arms around the newcomer, but his arms went right through her. "Shh, it's okay. Everything is okay."

To my intense dismay, the girl kept screaming. Darren's response at her ignoring him would have been funny in any less dire situation.

Finally shaking off my initial freeze response, I stepped toward her. Although I intended to calm her, her screams got louder. Word salad exploded out of me. Anything to make this moment better. "It's okay, it's okay. I found him like this."

"Help! Help!"

I took a deep breath, considering my options. Common wisdom said when someone was hysterical, slap them. There was no way that would help. The massage therapist stood between me and the exit, so running was out of the question. But Darren knew her. He'd might help.

"What's her name again?"

Darren looked sadly at the still-screaming massage therapist. "Eve. She's got hands like a goddess."

25

The salon owner burst into the room. It took me a minute to recall her name: Suzanne Bracken. She looked from Eve to me to Darren and gasped. To her credit, she recovered quickly, standing up tall and looking down her nose at me. "What's going on in here?"

Eve pointed. When she spoke, the words came out in a sea of hiccuping sobs. "She was standing over Darren's body."

"He was dead when I found him." Neither of them was listening to me.

"I... went... oil... and... Darren! He's gone... She was going through his pockets! She must have killed him."

A horrified gasp escaped Suzanne. Both women turned toward me. To be fair, assuming that the strange woman searching a dead man's belongings killed him wasn't an enormous logical leap, but there was no evidence of murder. He could have died a million different ways.

My belief that it might be poison meant nothing, especially since it was based on Darren's physical symptoms, which I couldn't possibly know. Until a medical examiner weighed in, I needed to proceed as if this were a natural death.

"Oh, no, it's not like that," I blurted. "I heard something, so I came in. He was dead when I got here. I tried CPR, but it was too late. I didn't touch him. Except the CPR. You can't do CPR without touching someone."

Stop babbling, Emma, I told myself.

Suzanne crossed her arms. "Were you going through his pockets?"

"I was looking for his phone to call for help. Mine's in the locker room. I knew he had his because he was using it in the Relaxation Room."

The younger woman gasped. "That's right! You asked

Missy to throw him out! And when it didn't work, you killed him!"

The ghost snorted. "That's what you get for refusing to help. Now they think you killed me."

I shot him a look and lowered my voice. "Do you really think this is funny?"

Suzanne put her arms around her employee, who sobbed hysterically against her shoulder. "There, there, Eve. This is quite a shock. Come with me. I'll get you something that will help you feel better."

"I don't want to feel better!" she wailed. "I want Darren!"

Suzanne turned Eve toward the door without her gaze ever leaving me. "I don't know what happened, but I'm going to call the police."

"I'll come with you," I said. "I can give a statement."

"He was alive when I left," Eve burst out. "How could you?"

Suzanne said, "Go wait in the Relaxation Room where we can monitor you. I'm sure the police will want to question you. Don't leave. We have excellent security."

Where was I going to go wearing a bathrobe? In my rush to respond to Darren's calls for help, my weird rubber spa shoes got left behind. All my other stuff was in a locker at least four rooms away, including my car keys. Presumably, security would be alerted to stand guard before I got there. Unless I wanted to walk several miles with no shoes, no clothes, and my face and body covered in a honey-based wrap, I'd be staying put.

That reminded me: my locket was still in the dish in Missy's room. That locket belonged to my dead grandmother, and it was my only way of bringing my long-long dead grandfather with me when leaving the mansion. It was also one of the first big magic spells I'd accomplished, so wearing it made me proud. While the trinket might not be worth a lot of money, it was irreplaceable.

How could I ask two women who thought I killed a man to take me to get jewelry? That looked as bad as searching Darren's pockets for his phone. Or touching his linens to find out what happened and leaving trace evidence.

Darn it. With Darren distracting me, I hadn't been able to finish my conversation with the sheets. They might have provided valuable information, and it was too late now. Unless I could tell Suzanne my intent to get my necklace, double back and... what? Ask the police processing the crime scene if I could touch a few things?

Great idea if I wanted them to arrest me.

The three of us returned to the Relaxation Room, with me in front and Suzanne consoling Eve. There was no opportunity to slip away. Before I could ask about getting my necklace, Suzanne directed me to the nearest chaise. Figuring cooperative could only make me look better, I complied.

Suzanne left to call the police. With another dirty look at me, Eve stalked to the far corner and settled onto a lounge chair. Darren's ghost followed her. It seemed odd that he wouldn't stay with the only person who could see him, but maybe he wanted to know if Eve killed him.

Missy sat and put her arm around Eve. A few other guests napped or read on their chairs, blissfully ignorant of what had happened not far away.

No way was I going to relax now. Like it or not, I'd encountered another ghost at loose ends. Darren needed me. He'd probably been poisoned, something the police would eventually discover. Since I'd been found in the room with him, it looked like I did it, and I'd stupidly given myself a motive when reporting Darren's rudeness.

Darren had been lying on the massage table on his back. Alone in the room. Where was Eve? She'd been distraught when she returned, but why had she left? Where did she go?

Why would a massage therapist leave in the middle of a treatment? While my procedure included alone time to marinate, a massage was a much more hands-on proposition. In my experience, the service took up the entire time allotted, and the massage therapist remained present— massaging—from start to finish. Eve said something about needing oil, but she should've had a supply on hand.

I didn't see Eve walking out on Darren mid-service without a good reason. Especially if she was used to him tipping well, like Missy said. He seemed to like her, so I'd be surprised if he'd driven her away with rudeness.

Based on Eve's reaction at finding me standing near Darren's body, she wasn't likely to answer questions for me. There must be another way to get answers. I was a thread witch, and this place was full of linens.

Sending my power out, I sought the sheets on the table where Darren had lain immediately before his death. This would be easier with direct contact, but I'd been practicing. My range wasn't super far—I couldn't get to my neighbor's house, for example. But any fabric within about fifty feet usually responded to me.

There they were. Not just linens, but ones with impressions of Darren. The threads were confused, scared.

Everything's okay, I told them. *No one is going to hurt you. Can you tell me what happened?*

The feelings returned by the sheets gave me the opposite of what I'd expected. Prior to his death, Darren had apparently felt something stronger than your typical masseuse/client relationship. Given the way Eve reacted to his death and Darren's attempts to console her, that wasn't a complete surprise. But if she was the other person in the room when he died, she shot to the top of the suspect list.

The threads held potent emotions: love, attraction, fatigue, frustration, and a hint of nausea. As if Darren wasn't feeling well physically, but cared about whoever he was thinking about.

This type of establishment didn't seem the sort to offer "happy endings." Suzanne would be beyond offended if I asked her about it. So would Eve. Something was definitely going on between them, but I'd have to ask Darren.

Based on the way he felt before entering the massage room, it sounded like he couldn't have engaged in hanky-panky—but maybe there had been something during previous appointments. Maybe he'd tried to be amorous and wasn't feeling well enough.

Pulling memories from thread wasn't an exact science. It didn't work on ghosts because they didn't wear physical clothes. I'd get more from touching the fabric, but the paramedics would be here any minute. If someone caught me in there a second time... the thought made me shudder.

Taking a deep breath, I reached for my magic again. This time I searched for any threads that recently felt anger. It only took a moment to get a response: from Suzanne's silk blouse. A murdered client would torpedo the business; it seemed unlikely that the spa's owner killed him on the massage table in a fit of rage. Even if she hated Darren, she could have killed him anywhere else. But I filed that information away for later. Maybe this wasn't planned. Heat of passion killings didn't have to be logical. If Suzanne walked in on Darren and Eve in a compromising position, that explained Suzanne's anger.

I didn't pick up any other powerful emotions except a deep sadness coming from Eve. Much as I strained, none of the fabrics gave me any sense that the person wearing them was anxiously waiting to hear if their dastardly deed had been successful. The killer either wasn't in this room or wasn't thinking about Darren's death.

Again, not a science. I'd have to talk to people if I wanted to learn anything.

While I was trying to think of an excuse for starting a conversation with Suzanne, the door to the locker rooms opened. Detective Timothy Pratt entered with a uniformed officer I recognized as S. Gutierrez from an encounter at my home a few weeks ago. If I'd ever learned what the S stood for, I didn't remember.

The Willow Falls Police Department wasn't terribly large. Probably about half a dozen officers. Detective Pratt was, to my knowledge, the entire homicide department, so seeing him shouldn't have come as a surprise. I took in his graying waves and piercing brown eyes, surprised to feel a smile coming onto my face. We'd gotten along well until he'd arrested my only friend, and seeing a familiar face brought me comfort. Especially because he reminded me of a 1995-era James Bond. Who doesn't feel safer with Agent 007 around?

Stepping into a spa's tranquility-themed resting area wearing a suit, tie, and dress shoes should have made Detective Pratt look like an imposter. Instead, we all suddenly seemed incredibly underdressed. I became uncomfortably aware that I still wore the spa's standard-issue bathrobe. Officer Gutierrez tugged at the collar of his blue police uniform, looking as awkward as I felt.

The officers commanded the room's attention by turning the lights up. Standing in the doorway, Detective Pratt loomed over those of us on the chaises. "Excuse me, everyone. I hate to interrupt your spa day. There's been an incident. All services are canceled until further notice. Mrs. Bracken will contact you about rescheduling. Meanwhile, I'm going to ask everyone to indulge me a bit and sit tight. We have some questions for everyone. Please do not leave without speaking to me or Officer Gutierrez here."

He spotted me instantly, probably because I started fidgeting with the belt of my robe. It wasn't until after I'd flushed and dropped my hands that I remembered I could have just asked the darn thing to stay closed.

"Oh, no. You're not going to flirt with the detective investigating my death, are you?" Darren asked, popping up beside me. "Some ghost whisperer you are. Next, you'll be pulling out a mirror and smoothing back your hair or adjusting your robe to give him a peek. Don't distract him. He might miss an important clue."

"It's none of your business, but we're just friends," I hissed out of the corner of my mouth. Louder, as Detective Pratt approached, I said, "Hello, Detective. I'm sorry to see you again under these circumstances." The movement made my cheeks feel weird, like the skin was cracking.

"We've really got to stop meeting like this. What happened to your face?"

Oh, no. The mask. Instead of the twenty minutes intended, it had been on probably at least half an hour. I'd completely forgotten Darren's earlier comment. I closed my eyes against the embarrassment. "Face mask. I was doing a body wrap when this happened. I never got to wash it off."

No need to mention the clay still coating my body, working its way into uncomfortable places.

"Hold on a sec." He went to Suzanne and said something into her ear. She signaled an attendant and nodded my way.

A minute later, a guy in his twenties appeared and handed me a warm, wet washcloth. I rubbed it over my face gratefully, wishing I could do the same with the rest of my body. "You're the best. Thanks."

"Don't mention it." He took the washcloth back and handed me a hand towel, which I used to pat my face dry.

"I don't suppose I could shower before we continue?" This question was directed at the detective.

He shook his head. "Unfortunately, no. I need to ask you some questions while everything is fresh. I understand you're the one who found the deceased. Is that right?"

"Unfortunately, yes," I said. "If I never see another dead body again, it'll be too soon."

"Amen to that." He took in the scene, his officers separating patrons for questioning, techs collecting evidence and putting up tape around the chaise Darren had used earlier. "If I didn't know better, I'd think someone wanted to make your life difficult."

A few weeks ago, I'd been at the center of another murder investigation, so I understood what he meant. "I know this looks bad."

"Bad? Why? Just because you were alone in the room with a dead man? Why would that look bad?"

Even knowing how the circumstances reflected on me, hearing Detective Pratt say he considered me a suspect sent a chill down my spine. After my closest friend in Willow Falls had been accused of murder a few weeks ago, the thought of going through another murder investigation exhausted me.

"Please tell me you don't really think I had anything to do with this. Not after I spent all that time solving your last case."

"We don't think anything yet. I don't even know what this is. I've been here for three minutes. For all I know, the man had a heart attack. Techs are going over the room now. I'm gathering information. But your presence near the body is one thing that makes the incident look suspicious. Why were you with Mr. Cartwright?"

He would never believe the actual answer, so I lied. "I was looking for the bathroom."

Detective Pratt's gaze went over me, taking in my white robe and extremely tousled red waves. His gaze made me feel warm all over. "What were you doing here?"

"This spa has excellent reviews. I wanted to try it. After all the stress of opening the bed-and-breakfast, it seemed like a nice way to take a break. I never had much money before moving to Willow Falls, and I thought—why not treat myself?"

"Take me through your morning." He sat on one of the lounge chairs and gestured for me to do the same. "Everything that happened since you arrived."

Step-by-step, I went over my day, starting with my arrival at the spa. He stopped me when I got to Darren's entrance into the Relaxation Room.

"Hold on. You noticed him?"

"Of course I did, Detective. He's got a big presence. He's muscular and loud. Everyone noticed him. He acted like he wouldn't have it any other way." Nervously, I glanced toward the corner where Darren still sat with Eve. It didn't look like he'd heard me.

"Sounds like you didn't like him."

"I didn't know him." I shrugged. "The one time I attempted to interact with him before he died, he ignored me completely."

He cocked his head. "That sounds like you tried to talk to him after he died."

"Well, I did CPR. Or I started to. His mouth did not look right." *Nice one, Emma. He definitely won't think you're hiding something now.* Time to change the subject. "Where was the massage therapist?"

"You know I can't tell you."

"Fine, don't. Isn't it strange that Eve was out of the room when her client was killed on the table? Did she get a phone call? Or maybe she knew what was going to happen, and she wanted to create an alibi." Now that I thought about it—where had Missy gone? Once she left me to chill, she had twenty minutes to do anything she wanted. Maybe she stole Eve's massage oil first thing this morning, then snuck into the room to murder Darren when Eve left to get it. For that matter, either of them could have dropped something in his tea. Everyone was a suspect.

"Thanks, Detective Faden," he said dryly.

My cheeks grew warm. "Sorry, I just want to help. You know, prove it wasn't me."

His smile transformed his face. His good looks stood out more when his gaze wasn't full of suspicion. "Anything else you haven't mentioned yet?"

"Well, yes, actually." Although we were already speaking quietly, I moved even closer. A faint whiff of sandalwood aftershave reached my nose. "I believe some services Eve provided to Darren weren't *on the menu*, if you know what I mean."

He raised an eyebrow at me. "If you're saying what I think you are, that's quite an accusation. You could get this place shut down."

"Then please don't tell Suzanne I'm the one who brought it to your attention," I said. "But I wouldn't say anything unless I was positive. Maybe there was a lover's quarrel, or maybe Suzanne found out about them and threatened to fire Eve."

"That sounds remarkably like wild speculation."

"They were definitely involved. Ask Eve."

"How do you know?"

I averted my gaze. "I'm sorry, I can't tell you."

"If you want me to act on a tip, I need more. Otherwise, it sounds like you're distracting me from the fact that you were standing next to the body, going through the victim's pockets."

"Can't you tell people you have a confidential informant like they do on TV?"

"I can." He crossed his arms. "As soon as you convince me you know what you're talking about. CIs have to be trustworthy."

I sighed. There was no way to explain that my magic told me about Darren and Eve's relationship. My room had an entire hallway away, so I couldn't pretend to have heard them. Maybe I could quickly rearrange the vent system to connect the two spaces... Right. The last time I used magic for a big remodel, it backfired loudly and nearly took out the entire building. I'd been fortunate to undo the spell with minimal damage.

"That's what I thought," he said.

"I can prove it. Just give me a little time, okay?"

"Haven't we already talked about you interfering in an investigation?"

"It's not an investigation yet," I pointed out. "There's no cause of death."

He shook his head. "Yeah, yeah. Still, stay out of it. I need to interview everyone else. Don't go anywhere."

I gestured at my robe, under which I still had no clothes. "Not an issue."

"Is there anything else you want to tell me?"

My mind went back to my earlier conversation with Darren. "Tell them to test for poison. His lips looked weird."

"Aren't massage rooms dark?"

"I tried to do CPR. Got real close before deciding not to put my mouth on his. But I promise, I didn't poison him. If I did, I wouldn't mention it."

The tips of his ears turned red. "Sorry. I'm just doing my job. My gut says you're not a killer, though, and my gut is usually right."

"Careful, you'll make me blush," I said teasingly. "That may be the nicest thing you've ever said to me."

"Don't let it go to your head. You're definitely hiding something, and I have every intention of finding out what. But I don't think you murdered anyone."

Killer? No. Witch? Yes. Ghost whisperer? Maybe.

"Thanks. You, too." Possibly the dumbest thing I could've said, but he had that effect on me.

"One other thing." He cleared his throat. "I owe you an apology."

"Nah. I know how suspicious I must've looked when Eve walked in."

"Not that." He looked me squarely in the eye. "For Josie."

"Ah." A few months ago, he'd arrested my best friend for a crime she didn't commit. That certainly put a damper on our relationship.

"I want you to know I'm a better cop than that. I don't arrest people without evidence."

"Then what happened?"

He sighed. "Her ex-husband has friends on the force. He put pressure on our crime tech. The man lied about the test results. I should have double checked, but Chief Yu got involved. It's the chain of command. Something felt off, but I told myself I didn't like how upset you were, and not to let my emotions impede an investigation."

"You care about my feelings?" The thought made me smile. But, despite the apology, this man arrested my friend. "How do I know you won't let someone talk you into arresting me next time?"

He closed his eyes for a moment before replying. "Because I would quit first. I already told the chief. She fired the tech, and she feels as bad as I do."

Since he seemed sincere, I decided to let him off the hook. "Thanks. If I think of anything else that might help, I'll let you know."

"I appreciate that. Oh, and Emma?"

"Yeah?"

"My friends call me Tim." He let out a shy smile before heading back to the uniformed officers.

Darn it, I'd meant to ask if I could visit the locker room to get dressed, but his comment sent all rational thought out of my head. Friends, me and the detective? Or maybe something more?

Given how we'd initially met, I hadn't considered the possibility, not least of all because I'd been interested in someone else. Juggling multiple partners, or potential partners, never appealed to me. Besides, he was a police officer. That made him an actual adult. One of those adulty people who had their lives together. The opposite of me.

But Detective Pratt—Tim—had a rugged handsomeness and self-possession I found attractive. Sparks flew when we got into a conversation. Did we have similar interests? Would we have things to talk about other than murder?

While I pondered these and other questions, Darren's ghost found me.

I leaned back in my lounge chair and glanced around. No one appeared to be paying any attention to me. Might as well ask about the rumor I started.

Trying not to move my lips, I whispered, "Darren, what were you doing before you died?"

"Well, I was on a massage table, naked, so obviously I was skydiving." He rolled his eyes. "They can't give me a smart guide to the afterlife?"

I forced myself not to respond with the same rudeness.

"Unfortunately, you're stuck with me, so it would help if we could work together. I pulled some impressions off the sheets, and it appears you were experiencing some romantic feelings shortly before your death. Was Eve, um...?" There was no non-awkward way to ask, so I spit it out. "Was she giving you a happy ending?"

He drew himself upright, nose in the air. "That is none of your business."

"You're right," I said. "But if you were engaging in relations with someone who killed you, it would help to know who to investigate."

"She would never!" he said. "Eve loved me."

That gave me pause. "You were in a relationship?"

"You thought she slept with all of her clients?" Darren looked offended on Eve's behalf. "But to answer your original question, nothing happened today. I started feeling weird in the hallway. We talked for a bit, and then she offered me a massage to help me relax. When she couldn't find oil, she left. I fell asleep. Then you came in."

My eyes went to his left hand. No wedding ring. But a slight indentation surrounded the fourth finger. The skin was a lighter color, as if he normally wore a ring. Tan lines didn't lie.

"You're married?" I asked. "To Eve?"

"No!" Quickly, he amended. "I mean, yes, I'm married. Not to Eve."

"Did she and your wife know about each other?"

"Why are you so interested in my personal life?"

Okay, he obviously didn't want to talk about the cheating. We'd come back to that.

"In the vast majority of murders, the victim knew their killer. Can you think of anyone who wants to hurt you?"

"My agency is very successful, so don't go thinking I got killed for owing someone money."

That was weird. I didn't even know how to respond, other than changing the subject.

"In the Relaxation Room earlier, you were on the phone," I said. "It didn't sound like the conversation was going well. Who were you talking to?"

He sniffed. "A business associate. Claimed a competing agency made a better pitch. They'd go with them unless we reduced our price. I refused, naturally. A deal's a deal. They signed with us. Use the ad or not, but they're paying for it. The guy might have wanted to kill me when we got off the phone, but he never could have made it here so fast. That's if he knew where I was, and he didn't."

I took a deep breath. "Do you know if you had other business associates or maybe an employee who would hurt you?"

"You're asking a lot of questions. What do you care, anyway?"

If Darren was going to change the subject every time I came close to the question of who might have wanted to kill him, this inquiry would take forever. However, since the guy had just died, I cut him some slack. "When you realized you were dead, I heard your screams. I thought a living person needed help, so I jumped up and went to find you. No one else in the building can hear ghosts, apparently. My grandfather could have, but he's gone. Besides, he's also a ghost and can't tell anyone what happened, either." I resisted the urge to shake my head at my babbling. When I got nervous or stressed, random words started tripping over themselves in a race to exit my mouth. "Anyway, I ran into the massage room to see who needed help. Eve found me standing beside your dead body. She and her boss think I killed you."

"Why would you want to kill me?"

Because you're overbearing and obnoxious? Gritting my teeth, I said, "I didn't."

"So you claim. I don't remember what happened. Why should I trust you? I didn't become a successful salesman by taking people at their word."

Enough was enough. There was plenty for me to investigate without wasting time arguing with a ghost.

"Fine. Don't trust me," I said. "Figure out how to get to the afterlife on your own."

"Maybe I will. Then you'll be sorry."

Before I could think up a sufficiently scathing response, he vanished.

CHAPTER

SIX

Well, this grandfather-granddaughter bonding experience was going splendidly. I'd lost Walter, been caught stealing from a dead man, and offended the only person who could clear my name. All while covered in goop and wearing a bathrobe that didn't cover as much as I'd prefer.

I should have stayed home and binged cooking shows on Netflix. Instead, I was trying to figure out how to ask a heavily armed stranger for permission to shower and get dressed.

The locker room was down a short hallway from where we waited. So close, yet so far away.

At the reminder of how little I was wearing, my fingers went to my bare neck. I had a more immediate concern: getting back my priceless locket. If it disappeared forever, Walter would be crushed, and I would never forgive myself for taking it off.

Missy's room was pretty close to the place where Darren's body lay. Maybe I could sneak over, go in with no one noticing, and get my necklace back. The murderer

43

wasn't hiding in there. The police shouldn't care about it. If they did—well, even if I had murdered Darren, he wasn't attacked with antique jewelry.

Enough sitting around. I was getting my necklace. Maybe putting it on would bring Walter back to the spa. Even though I'd bound Walter's ghostly form to the locket so he could leave the mansion, I was still pretty new to magic. It hadn't occurred to me I'd lose my companion by removing the locket. I needed to see if he came back.

And if I passed close enough to Darren's room to over-hear anything valuable, great! Win-win. There was just the small matter of leaving undetected.

Note to self: look into invisibility spells. Maybe I could weave a cloak.

Two officers blocked the doors leading to the locker room. Although I wondered if they'd let me get my clothes, my outfit wasn't a priority. Detective Pratt was nowhere to be seen: he must have gone to the crime scene. Suzanne sat on a chaise near the corner, possibly the least relaxed anyone had ever been in that position. With her face full of storm clouds, she tapped furiously. The police must have asked her to help them find security footage or something. Whatever she was looking for, she didn't seem to be happy about it.

Missy sat with two other women and a man in similar outfits to hers. Everyone with long hair wore it pulled back neatly. I couldn't see name tags from here, but they must all be staff. One looked like the woman who'd checked me in this morning, a hundred hours ago.

I thought about how Missy had left me alone in the massage room. A coincidence? Where did employees go while customers relaxed during a treatment? I wondered if anyone had seen her, or if she'd spotted Eve outside of Darren's room.

Well, that's what the police did. I'd given Detective Pratt my statement. Let him follow up. All I wanted was my locket. Then a shower and my clothes.

A non-uniformed police officer interviewed another guest, who I identified because she also wore a fluffy white robe and plastic shoes. A handful of similarly attired people sat nearby. One woman was reading. I applauded her ability to ignore what had happened and focus on her book.

No one was paying any attention to me. That could change any second, so I needed to move fast. The beverage station serving tea and coffee wasn't far from the side exit. That hallway went to the room with my locket. I headed for the counter, thinking it would be easier to slip away if I pretended to get a drink first.

"Ma'am?"

The officer's voice stopped me dead in my tracks. I hated when people called me ma'am. It made me want to check for my grandmother. Instead, I pivoted to face Officer S. Gutierrez. The younger officer had short, spiky black hair, brown eyes, and an extremely unfriendly expression. Apparently, he didn't remember my first name, either.

"Emma," I said.

"Officer Gutierrez," he replied. "Where are you going?"

"To get a drink?" I didn't know how that became a question.

He shook his head. "Sorry, I can't let you do that. We have a dead man, and no one has determined the cause of death. I can't let you consume anything."

Right. That was why I wasn't already drinking the tea. Because it was probably poisoned, and I didn't know where that happened between the initial brew and Darren's cup.

But Officer Gutierrez couldn't know I'd lied about my mission.

I opened my eyes wide and blinked at him rapidly. "Oh, wow, really? Thank you, Officer! You may have saved my life!"

"I wouldn't go that far," he said nervously. "I was about to take the container to get tested. Meanwhile, we'll get bottled water in here. Unopened."

After another overly effusive thank you, I headed for a lounge chair beside the exit. As soon as he turned to speak with the second officer guarding the main doors, I disappeared. The carpeted hallway muffled my footsteps, thanks to a handy spell my teenage self would have given anything for.

With all the doors closed, it was impossible to recognize Missy's room. Earlier, she led the way, in dim lighting, with Walter talking my ear off. My primary focus had been not to appear like I walked around having conversations with myself.

It was a constant struggle.

Too bad he'd vanished. Walter would have remembered which room it was. After so many years trapped in the mansion, he committed every detail to memory.

There had been a picture on the wall, maybe? Not helpful, since calming landscapes hung everywhere. The one by Missy's room definitely depicted mountains. Or a beach. Or possibly a meadow. As did every single painting.

About three yards down the hall, I spotted one that looked familiar. With nothing else to go on, I opened the door and ducked inside.

Inside, a spa employee sat in the middle of the massage table, head in her hands. Her shoulders shook. Although I couldn't see the woman's face, her long dark hair was pulled back like the other specialists, and she wore the same soft cotton black pants and top.

When I entered, she looked up. Eve. I didn't realize she'd left the Relaxation Room. She must've wanted to be alone. As soon as recognition dawned, she took a deep breath, preparing to scream again.

I held up my hands. "I'm not going to hurt you."

"Why should I believe you?"

"I know how this looks, but I didn't kill anyone. I never met that man until ten minutes before my massage."

"You were sitting with him in the Relaxation Room."

"He barely looked in my direction. He was on the phone, talking about a contract. It sounded serious."

She smiled sadly. "It was so hard for Darren to relax."

"I'm sorry for your loss," I said, deciding that my necklace could wait a few more minutes. This might be my only opportunity to question the last person who saw Darren alive. "Had he been a client long?"

Her eyes filled with tears, and I realized how red they were. She'd been crying, probably since we last spoke. This wasn't the sadness of a masseuse who had lost a client— whatever happened between them, it wasn't transactional. They seemed to care about each other. "You should go."

"Obviously, you don't trust me," I said, "but I'm on your side. I promise, I had nothing to do with this. Darren was dead when I found him. But I know you and Darren were engaging in services not listed on the website, and I thought you could use some comfort."

"You made it sound so tawdry. Not that it's any of your business, but he loved me. I know he loved me."

The way she said it made me wonder who she was trying to convince, me or herself.

"Was he acting oddly before the massage?"

"Why would he be acting strange?"

"Just asking. I wondered if he might have been sick." Or poisoned, but bringing that up would raise her suspicions.

She stared at me for an eon before answering. "He got dizzy in the hall. Said it was nothing, he hadn't eaten much for breakfast. He insisted he'd be fine once he got on the table."

"Was he, um, in a romantic mood once you got there?"

"Would you be feeling sexy if you wanted to puke?"

An excellent point. It sounded more and more like poison. "He didn't throw up, did he?"

"No." She paused. "What were you doing in the room? Why were you going through Darren's pockets?"

"I heard something, so I went to investigate. When you walked in, I was looking for his phone to call 911. Missy can confirm I was in her room a few minutes before you found me."

"Where was she?"

"She left me to relax while the wrap did its thing." If Missy had killed Darren, I should have passed her in the hallway between the two rooms. She could've hidden in another room—but how would she know which ones were occupied? "Is there a way into the building other than through the locker rooms? A back exit?"

"Sure. There are employee entrances. Suzanne doesn't want us in the client area in our regular clothes when we're rushing to get home."

"Is there one near your massage room? Because if there is, it's possible someone came in, killed him, and left. It could've been anyone."

"That's impossible," she said. "Those doors lock automatically. You need a code to get in."

"Does anyone ever leave one open by mistake?" Or even

on purpose, like a co-conspirator. I was grasping at straws, but if Darren's ghost returned, I wanted to give him answers.

She shook her head emphatically. "They close and lock behind you. Leaving one of those doors open is grounds for immediate termination."

So was killing a customer, I would guess. "What about a former employee?"

"The codes get disabled. It's the first thing Suzanne does. Sometimes even before we leave."

"I'm guessing no one would share their code with someone else?"

"Not unless they want to get fired. We're not even supposed to write it down, and the system assigns random codes so people who know us can't guess."

"Does anyone keep activity logs?"

She shrugged.

Interesting. Missy could have left, gone around the outside of the building, and come back through one of the employee entrances. Without records, no one would ever know. But so could anyone who worked here.

Eve was with Darren right before he died. She seemed genuinely upset at his death, but it would be naïve to keep assuming her innocence. People got killed for less than that. Including almost me, recently.

Hoping she didn't sense my suspicions, I asked, "Where were you?"

"What do you mean?"

"Darren was lying on the massage table, alone. You weren't in the room. Where did you go?"

"I ran out of massage oil. Usually, I fill it before I go home, but someone must have borrowed it. The bottle was gone."

"You didn't notice earlier?"

"Darren was my first client."

"Where do you keep that stuff?"

"There's a storage closet outside the locker rooms. It holds anything we might need."

Convenient that she happened to run out of oil in the middle of his appointment. Gave her a good reason to be across the building when someone found Darren's body. On the other hand, when she came back, she *had* been carrying a small plastic bottle.

"How long were you gone? Did anyone see you?"

She narrowed her eyes. "Why do you ask?"

Warning bells rang in the back of my head.

Quickly, I said, "Just trying to figure out where everyone was. If you saw a potential suspect, that might help. Just trying to cross people off the list."

"Right." She softened. "No one. I wish there was. I wish I knew how this happened."

Occam's Razor said that the most obvious explanation was usually true. Here, it seemed most likely that Eve killed Darren and waited for me to find him so she could act surprised.

My eyes went up and down her muscular forearms and I suddenly became uncomfortably aware that no one knew I'd come in here.

The police had asked everyone to stay in the main room. No one knew I'd left.

What if I'd isolated myself in a room with a killer?

SEVEN

Once the unsettling reality that Eve might have killed Darren dawned on me, this conversation needed to end. I reminded myself that I'd come to the day spa to relax, not to play detective.

Ha! As if I could relax now.

But I didn't need to investigate. The town of Willow Falls paid a fully staffed police department. Darren didn't want my help: he'd flounced away almost twenty minutes ago. Detective Pratt would sort everything out. Time for me to stop sticking my nose where it didn't belong.

I cleared my throat. "Anyway, sorry to bother you. I thought this was Missy's room. I left my necklace in there earlier."

She gestured to the right. "Missy's next door."

"Thanks." I left as quickly as possible without running, hoping she didn't notice my distress. I didn't breathe again until Missy's door shut behind me. I gulped air while trying to will my racing heart to calm. Eve was one of several suspects. I didn't have any evidence she killed Darren.

Still, I wouldn't feel better until I got back to the room full of police officers.

These interior doors didn't lock and weren't terribly sturdy, so closing myself in Missy's room offered little protection against a killer. But once I asked the carpet fibers to warn me if anyone approached, I felt better. As long as I got notice, my magic could protect me.

Once my pulse returned to normal, I took a moment to locate my locket. No one appeared to have touched the room since I left. The towels I'd magically tossed away still lay on the floor, by the walls. The table itself had traces of a clay body mask on it, and the remaining covers were rumpled. More importantly, my necklace lay in the gold dish on the counter, exactly where I'd left it.

A weight lifted from my chest as the necklace slid over my head. I looked around hopefully, but nothing happened. Walter didn't pop up. Too bad. Despite his inability to offer any physical protection, I felt safer when we were together. Ghosts made great lookouts. Also, I felt terrible for expelling him from the building.

I vowed to apologize profusely when I got home. Assuming the police let me leave sometime today. No one at the mansion knew what happened. Without my phone, there was no way to tell them. Josie would worry if I stayed too long after my appointment time, especially if she found out Walter returned without me. She couldn't see the ghost, but my cat could. She usually didn't understand Pink, but he could communicate when necessary. Part of cat magic.

Before leaving, I grabbed a towel and removed as much of the dried body scrub as possible. There wasn't a regular sink, and I didn't have the first clue how to use the torture bar/shower thingy Missy told me about, so that was out.

But this stuff was itchy, and I needed to feel as normal as possible.

When I made it back to the Relaxation Room, Detective Pratt had returned. He stood near the far wall, talking to Missy. She spotted me watching, and both turned toward me.

Awkward.

My cheeks grew warm. I averted my gaze and continued toward the nearest chaise.

Were they talking about me, or was I being paranoid? If Missy had returned to the massage room before Eve found me in Darren's room, Missy could help establish a timeline. Suddenly, I desperately wanted to hear their conversation.

Unfortunately, no matter how I strained, I couldn't hear them from where I sat. Moving closer now would look ridiculous.

Maybe there was another way. Closing my eyes, I reached for the threads of Detective Pratt's suit jacket with my magic. Silk lining, well made. Silk could be stubborn, not ideal for asking favors. But the outside was tweed, a subtly woven hound's-tooth that had been washed many times over the years, leaving it soft. Weaves were used to working together. Silently, I asked them to let me listen to what they heard. With a little prodding, the threads agreed.

This spell used a lot of power. It didn't last long, and I needed to see the target. The further away I was, the sooner I ran out of juice. Hopefully, I'd hear enough.

"Freeman, you say?" Tim asked.

"Friedman." She spelled it. "Missy Friedman."

"How long have you worked here?"

"About six years."

"Do you like it?"

"Mostly, yeah. Suzanne gives me plenty of shifts. The

hours are flexible when I need to pick up my kid. She lets us use the gym after everyone is gone. And one time, when my cable went out, she let my son use the spa's account so he wouldn't miss the Super Bowl."

Wow, that was nice of her. It didn't mean she wasn't a killer, but hearing something positive about her character made me think better of the spa's owner.

"Have you ever seen Mr. Cartwright before?"

"Who?"

"Darren Cartwright. Late fifties, stocky, dark hair. Carries himself like a mobster."

"Oh, yeah. Sorry. Never heard the last name. He's here a couple of times a week. Total jerk. So full of himself."

"You're not a fan, eh?"

She shrugged. "He's so rude to everyone."

Poor Missy. I reminded myself to add a larger tip to the bill when I checked out.

"What about Emma Faden? You know her?" Detective Pratt asked. "Medium height, long red hair, hazel eyes. Early forties."

At least they hadn't been talking about me earlier. I didn't feel great about them discussing me now, though.

Missy thought before answering. "She was my ten o'clock appointment. The woman who found the body, right?"

"Yeah. How did you—"

"Word travels fast," she said dryly. "Clients don't die every day. When I found out Emma was gone, I was afraid she'd been the victim."

I felt a twinge of guilt at worrying her, but there hadn't been time to tell her where I was going.

Detective Pratt said, "Why did she leave the massage room?"

"I don't know."

"That's not common, is it? For someone to leave when they're resting?"

She shrugged. "It happens. Sometimes a client has to use the bathroom mid-service. We tell them to go before, but not everyone listens. Darren would leave when he got a call, which was the worst. I swear that man couldn't relax if his life depended on it."

Her faux pas almost made a nervous giggle escape me, but I managed to contain it. Detective Pratt coughed. "Maybe it did. Where were you?"

"In the laundry room, folding towels. That's what we do when the client needs time alone."

"Was anyone else in there?"

"Not today. Just me and a pile of clean linens."

With a nod, Detective Pratt made a note. "Where is it?"

She nodded toward the locker rooms. "Connected to the locker room. Not far from the supply closet.

"Did you pass anyone?"

"I walked through this room. There are usually people here, but it's dark, so it's tough to recognize your own mother. I don't know if anyone noticed me. I didn't talk to anyone."

Interesting that Missy and Eve both claimed to be near the locker room, but neither saw the other. One or both of them might be lying.

"How tight are the blankets during a wrap? Could Ms. Faden have taken them off to sneak out, planning to re-wrap herself later?"

"Maybe, but she risked leaving a trail of clay body mask down the hall. If she planned to sneak out and kill someone, she wouldn't book the messiest service. And the wrap is pretty tight. To be honest, I'm surprised she got out of it without help."

"Can you walk me through what happened before you left Emma alone?" he asked.

As badly as I wanted to be understanding, this line of questioning made my blood boil. He'd told me he didn't think I was capable of committing murder, and there he was investigating me. I'd gone to help someone in distress, and now I was a suspect! See if I responded next time someone called for help.

Okay, fine, I would. But even though I understood things looked suspicious, it hurt to think anyone considered me a viable suspect.

Part of me wanted to ask all the threads in Detective Pratt's suit to detract, pinch his armpits. I tried to remind myself that the sooner they eliminated me as a possibility, the sooner I could go home.

I heaved a sigh, somehow catching the attention of the female officer waiting nearby. The town I lived in before moving to Willow Falls boasted over a million residents. Never had I met the same member of the police force twice. I'd lived here for two months and recognized every single officer in this room. This woman never gave me her name. In my head, I'd called her "Officer Rude."

Through narrowed eyes, she looked from me to Detective Pratt and Missy, then back. I didn't know if she'd figured out I was eavesdropping, but she headed right toward me. "We're letting people into the locker room to get dressed. One at a time. The boss thought you'd want to go first."

Ten minutes ago, this offer would have thrilled me. Now, I desperately wanted to stay and listen to this interview. But I couldn't admit that, and refusing to get dressed would look suspicious.

Surely I'd be much happier when not caked in mud. Plus, I'd feel less vulnerable once fully clothed.

She walked two steps behind me the whole way, checked the shower, and stood directly outside the curtain while I went in, hanging my robe on a hook on the outer wall. The officer bagged it for evidence.

"Why do you need that?" I asked.

"You touched the victim when you were doing CPR, right? Something might have transferred to you."

Seemed weird, but I couldn't argue. Instead, I turned on the water.

Most awkward shower of my life. Any other day, I would have lingered under the waterfall showerhead, taking my sweet time. Instead, after about thirty seconds of scrubbing the itchiest places, I did a quick rinse and turned the water off. My bathroom at home contained a very nice tub where I could be alone later.

Once I toweled off, she followed me to my locker and watched me take my clothes out. At least she turned her back while I dressed. She warned me not to turn on my phone before insisting I walk in front of her back to the Relaxation Room. At least I felt more comfortable back in my black yoga pants and light blue hoodie. Sitting in a room full of strangers in nothing but a bathrobe had left me feeling so exposed. Vulnerable. Even with nothing to hide, I didn't like it.

On the walk back to the Relaxation Room, I felt so much better, I barely noticed the sullen officer.

She deposited me inside the door, then moved over to S. Gutierrez and said something. He laughed.

Probably a coincidence, but the way his gaze flickered made me think she was talking about me.

Unfortunately, Detective Pratt was no longer talking to Missy. Any chance to hear the rest of their conversation was gone. I didn't see Missy at all, but as I looked around, my gaze landed on the spa's owner.

Suzanne glared at her open laptop. She was tall and willowy, with blond hair pulled back into a sleek chignon. Similar to the bun Eve sported, but fancier. Instead of the black cotton uniforms worn by most of the staff, she wore gray wool slacks and a silk blouse. When I'd arrived, she'd been pleasant, but not warm. She spoke with a soft voice and a big smile that didn't reach her eyes. The lines on her face suggested she was in her mid-50s. She had shown no emotion other than frustration from the moment Darren died. Anger, rage—could it all be to hide her guilt?

Before I had time to talk myself out of it, I strode over and settled onto the chaise beside Suzanne. Barely had my butt hit the fabric when her neck snapped up. "Do you mind? There are plenty of chairs here, and I'm very busy."

"I came to talk to you, actually. You seem stressed."

"Of course I'm stressed! A man died in my spa. If someone had alerted me quietly, I could have covered it up. We'd have taken him quietly out a back door. But stupid Eve, she started screaming—before I could do anything, she'd broadcast the news to everyone. How could she do that to me?"

Interesting that she was more concerned with the potential loss of business than the life extinguished. "Do people often die at the spa?"

"As if I would answer that. But it's not one hundred percent unheard of. There are procedures. There are forums for spa owners, and we talk about these things. I never considered a murder, though." She gestured down the hall and sighed. "This is my worst nightmare."

Her words rang true. As obnoxious as Darren was, the spa owner seemed furious that he'd been killed here. Even if she knew about Eve and Darren's relationship and *wanted* to murder him, doing it here seemed unlikely. Not when she could pull his address from the files or follow him to a more isolated location.

"This is a nice place, you know. I was really enjoying my time here."

"You don't need to butter me up. You'll get a full refund for today's services."

"Is that your only concern, the money?"

"Oh, no." Her head snapped up. Horrified blue eyes met mine over the laptop. "Please don't put that on Yelp. I'll give you coupons, anything."

"Suzanne, listen. I'm not here to sabotage your business," I said. "I just wanted to be sure that you understand I had nothing to do with this. It must have been quite a shock to find me and Eve in the room like that."

"If you'd done it, I'd give you a free membership for life." She snorted. "Darren was a first-class jerk to everyone."

I cleared my throat. "Um, Eve seemed to like him."

"Eve likes the big tips. Darren's a sweet talker, or he was. Getting the pretty young massage therapists to like him was a big ego boost. Before her, it was someone else. There would've been someone else after her. If any of those girls knew the real person, they wouldn't fall for his act. I keep telling Eve, 'He's in advertising. It's his business to make you like his product, and in this scenario, he's the product.' She never wanted to hear it." She heaved a sigh. "I was starting to think I might have to force him to see one of our male staff members. Eve's a sweet girl. She deserves better than a doomed crush."

While Suzanne spoke, I watched her face. It didn't seem like she knew about Darren's physical relationship with Eve. I didn't want to be the one to break the news. Suzanne would fire Eve on the spot, and she'd been through enough for one day.

The thought made my stomach churn. Weariness came over me. I was in over my head. Without Darren's help, there was nothing for me to do here, and he could be anywhere. I needed to go home and take a long nap. Detective Pratt knew where to find me if he needed to talk more.

After saying goodbye to Suzanne, I stood and scanned the room for Detective Pratt—er, Tim. He was talking to one of the uniformed officers who went to gather evidence in the massage room earlier.

When our eyes met, he moved toward me. I met him halfway. "Your number the same?"

"Yeah. Should I be expecting a call?"

He smiled for a second, then caught himself. "I may have some follow-up questions once I get your statement typed up. Can you come by in a couple of days, read over everything, and then sign it?"

"No problem. I'm happy to do whatever I can to help."

"Great, thanks. In that case, I'll have Officer Peterson show you out."

"Who?"

He nodded toward the corner and beckoned. Officer Rude. So that was her name. She beamed at him when he repeated the request. I didn't know her face could make that expression. Then he turned around, and she resumed her normal glare. "After you."

We walked in silence toward the front door. When we

arrived, Officer Rude crossed her arms and stared pointedly at the exit.

"Did I offend you somehow?" I asked.

"Offend me? Oh, no! Why would you think that?" If she'd been any more fake, she'd have to change her name to Milli Vanilli.

I sighed. "No reason. It doesn't matter. Have a good afternoon."

She didn't speak again until I'd passed through the door. "Your act doesn't fool me, you know."

"Excuse me?"

"There's something off about you, Ms. Faden. I plan to examine every single piece of evidence until I figure out exactly what you did to Darren Cartwright."

EIGHT

Officer Peterson's accusation stopped me in my tracks. I wasn't naïve enough to forget that finding the body made me look suspicious. Not to mention that I'd been going through the dead man's pockets. If they found poison in Darren's teacup, I might as well slap the cuffs on myself.

None of which I could say. The best thing was to avoid antagonizing her until some evidence pointed at a more viable suspect. Instead, I said, "Boy, will you be embarrassed if it turns out he had a heart attack."

Before she could reply, I hurried to the parking lot.

To my surprise, when I settled into the front seat of my battered old Toyota Corolla, a ghost leaned against the passenger side. I hadn't seen him when I walked up, but it wasn't Walter.

"Hello?" I called.

Darren slid through the door into the front seat, a sneer on his face. "Does this thing run? Can we take my car?"

"We?" After our last interaction, I'd figured he went

through his door without me. He seemed like someone who lived with no regrets.

His next words told me how wrong I'd been. "Of course, we. You've got to take me with you. You don't expect me to hang around the salon all day, do you? I'm a busy, important man!"

"Hold on. How are you coming with me?"

"Well, it's like this. You're the only person who can see or hear me, and I don't enjoy talking to myself. I'm staying with you until you fix this."

It was on the tip of my tongue to explain that fixing this situation would have nothing to do with making him undead. A friend of mine did that once, and she got into loads of trouble.

"That's not what I meant. You can't come with me. You have to stay at the spa," I said.

"Why?"

"Um... that's the rule," I said. "Isn't it? You stay in the place where you died. I think."

"Says who?"

The question gave me pause. I didn't actually know the answer. Who made these rules? My grandfather's ghost was tied to the place where he'd died, the family home he'd grown up in and lived in for almost seventy years. But Darren didn't live in the spa. He didn't appear to have any emotional attachment to it. It didn't make sense that he'd be stuck here forever. In fact, why was he here? Shouldn't he go somewhere more meaningful, like his office?

The only other non-relative ghost I'd encountered appeared near the spot where she'd died. She went through a door shortly thereafter, disappearing. There hadn't been time to experiment. Walter claimed to have unfinished business—what did Darren want?

Since I didn't have a good answer to Darren's question, I picked a bad one. "You can't come home with me. I've already got a ghost."

"I can't spend my eternal existence haunting a day spa! You think I want to watch spoiled, wealthy women get pampered forever?"

"At some point, the way I understand it, a door will appear. You open it, you walk through, and—Voila! After-life," I said. "Besides, you seem awfully judgmental for someone who was getting pampered at the same spa earlier today."

"That was different."

Of course. Everyone always thought they were the exception.

"What makes you so special?"

He clamped his lips together and turned toward the window. Right. He wasn't here for the ambiance. The spa provided a convenient place to hook up with his girlfriend.

"If you can leave the spa, why are you still hanging out with me? Don't you want to talk to your loved ones? Go see an old friend or two?"

"I tried. After you wouldn't help me earlier." He crossed his arms. "No one can see or hear me. It was embarrassing, trying to get their attention. My assistant looked right through me as if I didn't exist. She wouldn't have dared yesterday."

This might be the first time Darren had displayed anything resembling a genuine emotion since accepting that he'd died. "I'm sorry. That must be tough."

"Are we going to sit here yapping all day?"

So much for our touching moment.

Before we left, there was one more thing. Leaning

forward, I craned my neck to look for security cameras on the outside of the building.

"You won't find anything here," Darren said. "Suzanne's security system only recorded the lobby and other public areas, except the locker rooms. She wasn't worried about break-ins."

Interesting.

"If there was a camera in the hall or the room where you were killed, the police can pull the footage. They'll know if anyone snuck in."

"They can, but you said yourself: there's no sign of a struggle. The cameras would show me going in with Eve. She didn't kill me."

He seemed awfully certain of that. Her grief had seemed genuine, but I wasn't one hundred percent prepared to discount her as a suspect.

"You didn't overhear anything while you were alone, did you? See someone confessing into a mirror?" It was a long shot, but since we were still at square one, I might as well give it a shot.

"Nah. I went to see Eve; she was devastated. Crying on Missy's shoulder. Then I went back to Eve's room to get my phone, which I couldn't pick up."

"Sorry. I should've warned you. You can't affect the outside world. If you attempt to touch anything, or anyone, nothing happens. Like when you tried to hug Eve. You can, however, walk through walls, which you saw when you got in my car."

"I wanted to open the door. It didn't work."

"What did you see in there?"

"Inside your car door? I don't know, rust."

"No, at the crime scene. In the massage room." I took a deep breath. "Were the police gathering evidence?"

"Oh, yeah. Your detective friend was in there, checking me out for wounds. They found a red hair on my chest, probably yours."

Few people had the bright red shade my hair had settled into when I inherited my powers. If the strand belonged to me, Tim would know instantly. As would every other officer.

"Did they say what they thought happened?"

"Nah. They were gathering evidence. One of them called the coroner. She said it might take weeks to get results. Small town, you know."

Our county shared a coroner with Shady Grove, and she only worked part time. On the other hand, she usually didn't have many cases.

"It must be distressing to watch the police process the scene where you died." When Darren didn't respond, I asked, "Anything else?"

"I listened to the officers gossiping near the locker room doors. The female officer *really* doesn't like you."

"Yeah, I gathered that. Did she, by any chance, say why?"

"Something like 'I hate how Detective Pratt is all moony-eyed over that woman. She's always batting her eyes, and he comes running.'"

The thought of Tim having feelings for me brought a smile to my lips. "Maybe they weren't talking about me."

"She called you 'that red-headed hussy.'"

"Okay, that probably was me." My cheeks grew warm. "She really thinks he likes me?"

"Yeah. You want me to pass him a note after gym class?" He snorted. "This ain't high school. You like the guy, he likes you. Do the thing or don't, but don't pretend you haven't noticed how he looks at you. Even I saw it."

"In case *you* haven't noticed, he thinks I might be a murderer."

"Does not. He's just doing his job, and you know it."

We'd come full circle, from me giving Darren love advice to him returning the favor. Time to get out of here. "I'll keep that in mind. But I shouldn't sit in my car talking to myself much longer. I need to go."

"Don't let me stop you. I don't know why we're just sitting here, anyway. You can talk and drive, can't you? Let's see if this lemon starts! I've got things to do, places to go."

I raised my eyebrows. "Oh, yeah? Like what?"

"Don't act dumb. Writing ads! Wooing clients! Making money. I have a big pitch first thing tomorrow morning. There's a meeting with the team this afternoon to review everything, and we're about to be late."

How to put this tactfully? "You can't go to business meetings. You're dead."

Nope, that wasn't it.

"So? I told you, that's not going to slow me down. I have a business to run."

"That's not how this works."

"Excuse me? Then what am I paying you for?"

I blinked at him a few times, wondering if I'd somehow misheard him. "You're not. Do you think I'm one of your employees?"

"You said you were helping me. No one helps others for free."

"I do. It's my legacy." He snorted and muttered something I didn't need to hear. Ignoring him, I said, "When I mentioned helping the recently deceased with unfinished business, that didn't mean running an actual company on their behalf."

"Why not?"

"Because I don't want to." Not the best argument, but this guy's attitude got under my skin. I took a deep breath and released it slowly. "Listen, I'm sorry. It's been a terrible day."

"Says you!"

"Right. I know. It was nice to meet you. I wish I could help, but my role is limited to helping you move on, not teaching you better living as a ghost. Good luck with that. I wish you all the best."

"You're not going to handle my meeting?"

"Not to put too fine a point on it, but you've been rude and demanding since we met. Why should I help you?"

He grinned. "Because of my good looks and charm?"

"Try again."

Darren took a deep breath and started to sing. "It's fun to stay at the YMCA!" With each letter, his upper body twitched in the seat and his arms moved. What on earth was happening?

"Are you okay?"

He ignored me and continued singing.

Covering my ears and shutting my eyes, I counted to a hundred. It didn't help. Finally, I lost my patience. "STOP!"

He swung his arms from the 'A' position they'd been in to a crossing guard stance. "Collaborate and listen!"

If ghosts wore real clothing, Darren would find his suit growing upwards over his mouth. Since that wasn't an option, I gaped at him. "What are you doing?"

"Convincing you to take me with you. You were planning to leave the spa. You're supposed to help me. I don't want to stay here. You can't force me out of your car, and you wouldn't leave your car behind, so I'm going to sing until you change your mind."

Leave my car behind? An interesting idea. "You know what? I have changed my mind."

"Great!"

Before he could finish whatever he planned to say next, my door swung outward. Although returning to the spa later didn't appeal, I could take a walk.

I made it about halfway down the block before he caught up with me.

"Young man!"

"What?"

"There's no need to feel down." It took me a minute to realize he'd gone back to the beginning, but by the time we got to the chorus, I was having flashes of Village People.

It would have been easier to identify the lyrics if he'd been remotely on key. Compared to Darren's voice, fingernails on a chalkboard would be a joy. I'd rather listen to fighting cats while chewing tin foil.

Still, I kept walking. Darren spent all day bullying everyone in the spa, and I wasn't okay with that. Unfortunately, he was hard to ignore. Especially once he jumped in front of me, turned around, and started shouting again. Dance moves and all. You haven't seen disconcerting until a middle-aged, mobster-looking ghost gyrates while forming letters with his arms and screaming in your face.

It took all my resolve, but I kept going. Moving backward, he remained close enough that I could have touched him if he were solid. I would have gone right through him if he hadn't matched my steps.

We made it to the end of the block before I halted. It was "they can help you today" that did it. Darn everything.

I was supposed to be helping, not running. That was my calling.

Even though I didn't like Darren, I would help him

move on. Anything to end this poor excuse for singing. Well, except for actually taking over the agency and acting as his intermediary. I couldn't even upsell desserts to hungry people when I waitressed at the Olive Garden after high school. Coming up with catchy slogans and enticing images was miles beyond my skill set.

"Fine. You can come with me." If he was going to follow me around either way, I preferred he stopped singing. "But I don't think you'll be meeting with clients."

"Don't be stupid. You make the pitch. Negotiate the deal. With my help, of course. I need to make sure my partner doesn't run everything into the ground. He's useless without me."

We made it halfway back to the car before I said, "If I show up and tell your business partner that I'm your emissary, he might call the police. Considering that I am currently the number one suspect in your death, I'd rather not bring any more undue suspicion on me. If I'm going to help you move on, we need to clear my name first."

"Can't you do that on your own time?"

"Not really. I don't know you, your friends, your enemies, or anyone who might have wanted to harm you. Also, I'm not helping you unless you help me. Think of it as a business transaction. You like those."

"Deal." We shook on it. "Can we at least take my car?"

"Sure! I'd love to. Where are your keys?"

"In my locker," he grumbled. "I know where it is. I'll tell you the code."

As I slid back behind the wheel and put my key in the ignition—yes, my car was so old it still used a physical key —I shook my head. "Sorry, no way. Eve already caught me looking for your phone earlier. If anyone sees me going into your locker, or worse, driving your car, it's straight to jail for us. You could haunt someone else, but I'm no use to you behind bars."

"Then where are we going, Ms. Know-it-All? Will we make it alive in this heap?"

"You're already dead, so no." I patted the steering wheel of my old Toyota. We'd been through a lot together. "Don't you listen to a thing he says. You're a good girl."

"What's holding her together? Chewing gum?"

Er... magic, actually. Best not to mention that.

"You don't give up on a friend when they get old," I said.

"No, but you can upgrade to a newer model."

"Is that what you did with Eve? Upgraded?"

"Not exactly. I never intended to leave Angie."

"Did Eve know that?"

He looked aghast. "Of course she didn't know! Why would I tell her?"

"Depends on your relationship. If you had feelings for each other, it would be decent," I said. "If you were paying for her time, and it was all about the money, she wouldn't care. Not that it matters now."

"You're not going to tell her, are you?" he asked.

"How could I possibly explain knowing about your long-term intentions?" We were getting off track. "We still need to talk about suspects. What about your business partner?"

"No way," Darren said. "He's in California this week for a conference. Also, he's a schmuck."

A swing and a miss.

"Does anyone check people in when they arrive? Maybe he didn't really go."

"He's one of the featured speakers. Running sessions on wooing clients and other touchy-feely garbage."

"You're saying people would notice if he wasn't there?"

"I hope so."

"What about disgruntled employees? Anyone recently fired?"

"Uh, I got a new assistant about three months ago. My wife made me fire the old one for being too pretty. Thought I was going to have an affair."

"That's illegal."

"Well, don't tell Casey, then."

"Was she mad? Did she hold a grudge?"

He shook his head. "We gave her a year's severance to sign a release. That hurt. She decided to go back to school. Seemed happy."

"We should talk to her, just in case," I said. "Do you know where she lives?"

"There's an address in the HR file. May or may not be current. But we'd have to go to my office to get it."

Not in the middle of a weekday, we couldn't. "Fine, we'll talk to her later. What about your wife? Did she know about Eve?"

"Come on, I'm not stupid."

"Anyone else who might be upset with you?"

"Wait, yeah. Yeah, there was one guy we fired about two weeks ago. Barney."

"Why?"

"He was abusing our generous employee leave program. Always taking time off, leaving early, stuff like that."

Considering Darren already admitted to firing one employee for being attractive, I hesitated to ask the next question. "Was he sick? Taking care of a family member? Anything like that?"

"No. He was going to his kid's football games."

I gasped, clutching imaginary pearls for emphasis. "What a monster!"

"Fine, fine. Judge me. But when you're growing a business, you need employees who are dedicated to making it work. We can't wine and dine clients when people flit in and out anytime they want."

"Do you think Mr. Family Man held a grudge?"

"How should I know? We don't call former employees to ask how they feel about being fired."

The world might be a better place if more people did.

"Do you know where he is now?"

"Yeah, yeah. They called for a reference. He found a spot at Ed's Luxury Cars, down near Saratoga." Darren rubbed his hands together. "Oh, this'll be good! You go talk to him, and we get you into a decent vehicle."

"I don't need a new car." I turned my key in the ignition. Nothing happened. "That's a total coincidence."

Darren smirked at me. "Did you leave the lights on?"

"I don't think so," I said. "Sometimes you just have to be nice to her. Come on, girl, you can do it." I pumped the accelerator, although I didn't know if that would help. Then I turned the key again, holding my breath while I pressed my foot onto the pedal.

To my enormous relief, the engine roared to life.

"You look winded," Darren said. "Starting your car shouldn't be this much work."

Trying not to roll my eyes, I shifted into reverse. "Let's go talk to Barney."

When Darren mentioned a luxury car dealership, I figured they sold BMWs, maybe Lexus, with some electric cars thrown in. That barely covered the tip of the iceberg.

They had Mercedes, sure, BMW, Lexus, a couple of Tesla models up near the main road, and an adorable Mini Cooper. I even spotted a few Hummers. They also had brands I didn't even recognize because they were so far outside my realm. Gorgeous cars, very expensive, no idea who made them.

It wasn't just the vehicle selection. Everything looked luxurious, from the landscaping out front to the free espresso bar inside. When I bought my car (twenty years ago), I'd been impressed they'd set out a pot of stale coffee for customers.

The old Emma would have been laughed out of here. Now, even though I felt like an imposter, knowing I could buy every car on the lot propelled me through the doors.

My yoga pants may not scream "I have money," but attitude was everything. Fake it till you make it, right? I could do this. As soon as I stopped gaping at the massive chandeliers in the main showroom.

As I marveled at the marble floors, Darren said, "Close your mouth. They'll think you're so impressed, they can hose you on the deal."

"We're here to do recon. See if this former employee might be the one who killed you. I'm not buying a new car."

"Why are you so opposed?" Darren gave me what he probably thought was a friendly smile, but made him look like a shark. "Come on. I'll help you get a discount."

"I don't need a discount. I've got money. Probably more than you, now that I think about it."

He looked me up and down. "How do you think the rich stay rich?"

"Tax evasion and gerrymandering, mostly," I said automatically. "Ridiculously high salaries compared to your lowest paid workers?"

He gave me a withering look. "Because we hold on to our money. We don't spend it if we don't have to. By the way, that doesn't mean wearing clothes you've had for twenty years. Remind me to refer you to my wife's personal shopper."

"This is high-end athleisure! Moisture wicking fabric, doesn't stain or smell—"

My rant got cut off when a broad-shouldered, large man in a navy pinstriped suit broke away from the pack of salesmen and approached. His brown hair was neatly combed over the top of his shiny head, and he had friendly brown eyes. "Can I help you?"

"My name is Emma. I'm looking for Barney," I said.

"That's me. Nice to meet you." He held out a hand, and as we shook, I evaluated his grip. Firm. Solid. Could this man murder someone? And how would a handshake tell me?

"How did you hear about me?" he asked.

Deciding to keep my story as close to the truth as possible, I said, "I was chatting with a man at the spa this morning, and I mentioned my car is on its last legs. He suggested I come to you."

"Well, that was nice of him. If you don't mind my asking, what was his name? I'd like to send a thank you."

"Darren Cartwright."

Barney let out a guffaw. Then he stood up straight and tried to regain his composure. "Oh, wait. You're serious."

"I'm not that big a jerk," Darren said.

I gave him a side-eye. This wasn't *A Christmas Carol*, and it was too late for Darren to go back and behave better. But maybe he could still learn something.

To Barney, I said, "Yeah. Businessman. Fancy suit, loud voice."

"That's him. Darren referred you to me? Really?" He peered at me intently as if worried I actually was here on a secret undercover mission to take back his severance. If he even got any.

I swallowed. "Yeah. Like I said, I mentioned I needed a new car—" Darren snorted "—and he said if I wanted a serious upgrade to come to you."

"Why me, specifically?"

Although I didn't particularly want to tell the truth, lying didn't seem like it would benefit me. "He said you have kids and could use the commission. Also, that you're an old softie and would probably give me a discount."

Behind me, Darren chortled.

Barney smiled sheepishly. "I try to treat people fairly. Not that he knows what that means."

My ghost let out a sound of outrage, but I leaned in and lowered my voice. "Although I appreciate the referral, he seemed arrogant."

"You don't know the half of it," he said. "But I don't like to carry negative energy around with me. Let's talk about cars."

"There really aren't any hard feelings?"

"Hard feelings? No way. I love this place." He held out his arms and turned, gesturing at the surrounding lot. "Turns out, I'm better at matching people to cars than I was ads to products. I make my own hours, and when it's slow, they play Yankee games in the waiting room. I couldn't be happier."

"I'm glad to hear it." My gut told me that, whatever happened to Darren, Barney was not involved. He truly seemed happy and kind, not like a man twisted with anger. Also, he didn't seem aware that Darren was dead. "He felt bad about firing you. Said he was turning over a new leaf. I guess this is one way of doing it."

As Darren sputtered behind me, Barney led me into the lot, past half a dozen convertibles with a six-figure price tag. They were gorgeous, but I barely glanced at them. A convertible in Willow Falls made no sense. It rained half the year and was freezing the rest of the time. What would I do, build an indoor circuit?

Barney paused beside a gray sedan. It was nice enough, I guessed, but not terribly interesting. Four doors, windows. Looked like something Grandma Vera would've driven. "You got kids?"

I shook my head.

"How are you in the snow?"

"Umm, I got caught in a snowstorm once driving home

from vacation and almost slid backward down a mountain.”

“Yikes. I hope no one was hurt.” As I assured him that my friends and I survived the ordeal, mostly still speaking to each other, he took me to one of the smaller SUVs. It was bigger than what I was used to, but not so huge I’d feel like a soccer mom. And it had room for skis! You know, should I ever care to strap certain death to my feet.

“All wheel drive, leather interior. Handles like a dream.” He named a price much higher than what my grandparents paid for their house.

A nervous laugh escaped me. “Did you, by any chance, accidentally forget the decimal point?”

“Quality costs money. Darren wouldn’t have sent you if you couldn’t afford the best. Besides, I know who you are. Emma Faden?”

I nodded. “Have we met?”

“The whole town knows your name. You inherited Walter’s fortune, you’ve got a B&B that doesn’t have many guests, and your car is older than me.”

“Ouch.”

“He’s right,” Darren said. “Chew on that for a bit.”

“How often does it break down?” Barney asked.

“Um, can I plead the Fifth?” I sighed. “You’re right. You’re right.”

“It’s not just a new car. When people see a bed-and-breakfast owner driving something that’s falling apart, it makes them wonder how well she takes care of her business.”

“Also, when you show up asking questions about a murder in a rust bucket, people might wonder if you’re planning to steal from them,” Darren added, not helpfully.

In a show of defeat, I held up my hands. "You win. Get the keys. Let's go for a drive."

Barney grinned at me. "You won't be sorry."

An hour later, I still had no leads on Darren's murder, but proudly drove off the lot in a shiny new SUV. Somehow, I had been convinced to give up my beloved old Toyota. Not even I was immune to the siren song of this gorgeous blue Porsche Cayenne Turbo. I didn't understand when Barney explained what "Turbo" meant, and I didn't care.

Sliding behind the wheel, I ran my hands over the all-leather steering wheel and inhaled deeply. So that's what "new car smell" meant. Nice. Smelled like money.

"Good choice," Darren said. "I couldn't have done better."

"It is a nice car, but Barney didn't kill you. That's why we came here."

"You wanted to investigate Barney, and we did. Now people will take you seriously when you talk to them."

His attitude grated on me, but if his friends and associates shared his worldview, he wasn't wrong. "People shouldn't judge me by what I drive."

"Should or shouldn't, they do. Don't blame me, I didn't make the rules. What now?"

"Now, we should talk about other possibilities. We've just eliminated one of our most likely suspects."

"Yeah, Barney didn't do it. I forgot what a big, lumbering guy he is. I would've seen him at the spa."

"Maybe. We don't know how the killer got in. He doesn't seem to be angry that you fired him, though, or to have a malicious bone in his body. He also was a little too honest in his opinions. Usually people self-edit more when talking about someone they know is dead."

"Eh. Let's move on. What now?"

"Next, I thought I'd pay my condolences to your family. On the way, you can think about what you need to take care of before moving through your door."

He barked out a laugh. "Yeah, right. I'm not going anywhere, remember? I'm going to run my business and continue to build my fortune."

I hit the brakes and turned to look at him. "Why? You can't spend the money."

"It's not about buying things. It's about being the best. I don't see any reason to let death stop me."

My ghost refused to move on to the afterlife because he wanted to build his empire. Now I'd seen everything.

TEN

To get to Darren's house, first I drove to the east side of Willow Falls, the neighborhood nearest Vermont. Then, he directed me up a hill, past huge, open fields. My new Porsche handled like a dream. Until a couple of hours ago, I didn't even know Porsche made SUVs. Oh, but they did, and this one was amazing.

I didn't want Darren to see how much I loved my impulse buy, but—this was glorious. Bluetooth! Heated and cooled seats! It was sixty degrees out, but I had heated seats! Also, a heated steering wheel, which Barney assured me would change my life once winter hit. I was skeptical, but at least I'd be skeptical with warm hands. Plus, all-wheel drive and tinted windows and a backup cam, and self-parking.

Self-parking.

My car doors opened with an electronic doohickey, and almost everything inside was voice-activated. I was a little surprised the seatbelts didn't lock themselves. We had GPS in the dashboard!

The ride in this new car was so smooth, I barely noticed

my passenger's grumpy demeanor. Eventually, I stopped at the entrance to a massive gated community. The enormous gate glittered in the sunlight. The enormous *closed* gate.

A quick glance in my rearview mirror revealed no convenient car about to pull up behind me and use their own remote to let me in. There wasn't any car driving up from the other side, ready to exit and let me zoom in before the gates slammed shut. That always happened in the movies.

I pulled to a stop. "How do I get in? You didn't grab your gate opener before we left the spa, did you?"

"Don't sass me. Just input the code." He gestured to a metal box I hadn't noticed, although it couldn't have been more obvious.

"Are there cameras?"

"Probably. What are you going to do now?"

He had a point, so I typed in the four-digit number he gave me and waited for the enormous wrought iron monstrosity to swing inward. It moved exactly as fast as you would expect from a gate that weighed two tons.

About ten feet inside the gate, a sign informed me that the speed limit was twelve and a half miles per hour. "Half? How does anyone go half-a-mile per hour?"

Darren shrugged. "No one does. Lets the rent-a-cops stop almost anyone they want."

"I'll go ten, then."

We inched along. It took nearly five minutes of crawling past enormous properties before we reached our destination.

Darren's house made my mouth drop, and I lived in an old mansion. It wasn't just that it was big. Everything was so opulent. The McMansion dominated the lot, making it seem larger. Sculpted hedges separated the perfectly manicured lawn from the street. A giant driveway curved up to the front door and back, with a fountain in the middle. It had to be at least six feet tall, with four tiers of running water and a pond at the base.

The driveway sat empty, but most people parked in their garages because of the random year-round thunderstorms and vast amounts of snow. No one wanted to get drenched walking from their house to the car.

To my surprise, no police cars were parked out front. For a moment, I hesitated. If they hadn't been here yet, I didn't want to break the news about Darren's death to his family. Nor did I want another run-in with Officer Peterson should they arrive in the next half hour or so. On the other hand, it had been almost three hours since I left the spa, and the police had detained me after finding Darren's body. Someone must have contacted his family by now.

As soon as I pushed the button to turn the car off, my phone beeped with a text. Apparently, it had automatically gone into driving mode. I hadn't realized that was a thing. But it was, and Josie had sent me a message.

> Is everything okay? Your appointment was hours ago. You and T were supposed to go through Walter's trunks to find some warmer clothes before winter hits.

A wave of guilt hit me in the gut. In all the morning's excitement, I'd completely forgotten that I'd promised to help the newest resident at my bed-and-breakfast. The eighteen-year-old (whose legal name was Terrence) had been thrown out of his house a few months ago, and he owned almost nothing but the clothes on his back. He worked in the garden to pay for his room. T wouldn't let me take him shopping, but there was no need. Once my grandfather trusted me enough to reveal the hidden treasure trove of stuff in his basement, we had plenty of stuff that could be tailored in a snap.

Literally.

If T believed he and my grandfather were the same size, I saw no reason to educate him. He couldn't see ghosts, and Walter was happy to be remembered as six feet tall.

Quickly, I tapped out a reply.

> I'm so sorry. Something came up. Can you tell T I'll be home as soon as I can? I've got a stack of clothes in my sitting room upstairs. Just need him to try everything on when we get home.

I can, but he seems pretty bummed. That boy doesn't have many people he can count on.

> Way to twist the knife. :-)

I don't get to use my mom skills much, so I have to practice when I can.

> It's not my fault. I've acquired another ghost! Hoping a visit to his family will help resolve some issues. Can you make T some apology scones for me?

Way ahead of you.

I was about to ask if Walter had returned to the mansion, but if Pink wasn't around, I didn't want to open a can of worms. She'd just worry until one of us returned and spoke to Walter personally.

Taking a deep breath, I strode toward the front door with confidence I didn't feel. Even the gold door knocker shaped like a fleur-de-lis looked expensive. Who had knockers anymore? This one sat beside a smart doorbell. It must have used a motion detector, because I had barely raised my arm to grasp the gold handle when the door swung open.

"That's her," Darren said. "Angie."

Mrs. Angie Cartwright looked like the epitome of a rich wife. She wore a pressed, navy-pinstriped business suit that made her look like she should be running a bank. Expensive fabric, too. So soft you could curl up in it and take a nap. Her ivory blouse was real silk. Her makeup was perfect— freshly applied, according to the red rimming her eyes. She wore her graying blonde hair in an updo and looked at me over her wire-rimmed glasses like I was a child selling candy bars for the school soccer team.

"Can I help you?"

"Mrs. Cartwright, hi. My name is Emma. I came to talk to you about your husband."

She stiffened. "We are not paying you child support."

What? Ew.

Resisting the urge to roll my eyes, I shook my head. "That's not it. I was at the spa today when he passed. I'm so sorry for your loss."

"Thank you, dear." She sniffled into her handkerchief again. "Who did you say you were again?"

"My name's Emma."

"Just tell her the truth," Darren said. "She believes in all that hogwash."

"What?"

"Angie's got a psychic and everything. Oh, yeah! Tell her the psychic sent you."

As we spoke, Darren's wife watched me avidly, her eyes darting from my face to the air over my shoulder. There wasn't much to lose. Either I told her the truth, and she thought I was crazy, or I made up a lie and…she thought I was crazy.

I took a deep breath. "I have something unbelievable to tell you. But I have reason to believe you're fairly open-minded."

"Of course I am! But if you weren't having an affair with my husband, what are you doing here?"

A snort-laugh escaped me before I bit it back. "I'm a witch. I can see and talk to ghosts. Darren is with me right now. He wanted me to help you find the person who killed him."

Angie gasped.

Then her eyes rolled back into her head, and she fainted.

ELEVEN

"Smooth move, Ex-lax," Darren said to me when his wife slumped to the ground. "Did you know I thought of that slogan first? Then some—"

"You said to tell her the truth! She's supposed to be a believer!"

I rushed through the doorway to check Angie's pulse. It was steady and strong. She was breathing fine, too. Her chest moved up and down. That was something. I didn't see any blood, and nothing appeared broken. In fact, she seemed perfectly fine, just unconscious. She couldn't stay on the cold marble floor, though. I needed to move her without causing more damage.

"Apparently, she's a believer who never expected confirmation," he said.

"Thanks. That's really helpful," I said.

Angie was taller than me and while she was thin, I didn't think I could carry her without injuring both of us. Maybe I could splash water on her face or find smelling salts? That shouldn't be terribly difficult. The foyer smelled like a Yankee Candle.

Theoretically, I could lift her entire ensemble and float her into another room, but if anyone else was here, that wouldn't, er, fly.

Telling Angie the truth had been a terrible idea. I should have listened to my gut. Unfortunately, Darren's voice drowned out everything else and make it hard to think.

Now what? I didn't want to drag this woman across the highly polished marble floor, but maybe I could make her more comfortable. She'd probably wake up soon. Considering her reaction, I'd prefer she didn't remember what I'd told her when she did.

Inside a small, zippered pocket in my purse, I pulled out what looked like a sleep mask without elastic. The cloth had been spelled and treated before I'd cut it and embroidered symbols into the light blue fabric. The thread was also spelled, and if I'd done both steps correctly, I could make Angie forget what I'd said.

Placing the mask over her eyes, I whispered the words to erase the last sixty seconds. Many trained witches could do intense memory wipes, but I was still learning. All I could do was make someone forget a brief time period. Hopefully, it would be enough. I sensed the magic moving through the cloth, but Angie didn't move.

"What are you doing?" Darren asked.

"Memory spell," I said. "So when she wakes up, she doesn't remember me telling her I talk to ghosts. Either she was too fragile to handle it or she's not as open as you thought."

A door slammed on the landing above me. "Mom?"

A male voice. It didn't sound childlike, but Angie was at least fifty. To Darren, I hissed, "You didn't tell me you had kids!"

"I don't!"

"Then who's that?"

He grimaced. "My useless stepson. He claims to be 'between jobs,' so he moved back here. Probably ran out of money. I forgot all about him. We don't spend much time together."

If this man called the police, Tim would be furious to find me in Darren's home. I didn't know what else to do, so I called up the stairs. "Is anyone there? Can someone help me?"

"Hello? Who is that?" The voice drew closer.

Not wanting to be caught hulking over Angie's prone body, I stood and shoved the magical cloth into my pocket. I'd raised my hands so the stepson could see I posed no threat when he appeared at the top of the stairs and peered down at me.

"She fainted," I said. "I stopped by to pay my condolences, and I guess the strain of losing your stepfather was too much. I'm so sorry."

The guy raced down the steps, straight past me to his mother. When Darren mentioned a stepson, for some reason, I'd expected a teenager. This guy was younger than my forty-two years, but definitely not a child. No gray in his dark brown hair. None of the fine lines that formed when a person approached forty. I guessed he was about thirty. A few inches taller than me, with an athletic build. Hopefully strong enough to carry a thin middle-aged woman somewhere more comfortable.

While I examined the guy, he crouched down to check his mother for breathing and pulse, just like I'd done. "Did she hit her head when she fell?"

"I don't think so."

He hoisted his mother into his arms and headed toward

an open doorway at the rear of the hall. "Don't stand there. Close the door and follow me."

Not knowing what else to do, I obeyed. Darren trailed behind me. The whole time, I couldn't stop babbling. "I'm so sorry. I didn't mean to upset her. And I'm sorry for your loss, too. This whole thing is just terrible."

After placing his mother on the couch and arranging a couple of throw pillows behind her head, the guy turned to me. "It's okay. Relax. Mom has had a rough day. Her nerves were already shot. You were in the wrong place at the wrong time. By the way, I'm Ben."

"Emma," I said. "I should go."

"You should not!" Darren said. "We haven't learned anything yet. I'm telling you, this kid arrived last month in town and now I'm dead? Very suspicious. He never liked me, you know. He's not in the will, probably plans to take anything he can carry out of the house before the reading. Maybe he drugged his mother, and that's why she fainted."

"Yeah, sorry," Ben said. "Did you need something?"

I swallowed. "Your father—"

"Step-father." They spoke perfectly in sync.

Then Ben added, "Unfortunately."

"You weren't close?"

He snorted. "He was arrogant, self-involved, and completely uninterested in Mom's only child. Sent me away constantly. I hated him."

"You ungrateful snot!" Darren shouted.

I tried to shush him, but no idea whether he noticed. "Still, losing him suddenly must be a shock."

"I guess. Part of me isn't surprised. Darren knew how to make enemies."

My impression had also been of a long line of suspects,

but the confirmation gave me a sinking feeling. "How long was your mother married to him?"

"Almost twenty years," Ben said. "She's a saint."

Mentally, I added Ben's name to the list of people with a motive. He must have been a kid when Darren joined the family, but Ben didn't care that his stepfather had died. In fact, he almost seemed happy about it.

On the couch, Angie stirred. Ben went to her while I whispered to Darren to hush and let me interrogate his family. His constant interruptions made me dizzy.

"Mom? Are you okay?"

"Ben? Darling? I'm so sorry," Angie said. "What happened?"

"Let me get you some water," he said. "I'll be right back."

While he was gone, I introduced myself again and gave my condolences. Then I said I'd been asked to figure out what happened to Darren. Technically true.

"Can you think of anyone who might have wanted to hurt your husband?" I asked.

She sighed heavily. "No. I've been racking my brain since the police left. I already told them everything I know."

"Aren't you with the police?" Ben asked.

"I'm a private investigator," I said. It was sort of true. I was investigating. Privately. Just because my client was dead, and no one paid me, didn't mean it wasn't a legit job.

"What are you doing here?" Ben asked. "Do you show up and offer to help rich widows for a small upfront cash payment?"

"No! No, that's not it at all," I said quickly. "I'm not a scam artist."

"Tell them I'm paying you," Darren said.

"Your step-father hired me," I said. "A few days ago. He, um, was worried that something might happen to him."

Angie sat upright stiffly. "He never mentioned that to me."

"He may have been afraid you'd think he was weak," I said, eyes sliding to Darren. He seemed like the type of person who viewed any weakness as the worst possible trait.

Ben snorted. "Of course. Why let people know someone might kill you when you could die instead?!"

I smiled at him. "To some people, appearance is very important."

He glanced at his mother. "Yeah, I guess. Hard for me to understand."

Angie shook her head. Her eyes filled with tears. "Oh, my poor Darren. I can't believe he's gone."

"Listen, Angie, I know today has been very difficult for you." I pulled out a business card and offered it to her. "If you think of anything that might help, call me, okay?"

Angie sipped from her glass of water, placed it on the table, then focused her attention on me. "And who are you?"

That gave me pause, but she'd had a rough day. After all, her husband died. For the third time, I introduced myself. "I'm very sorry for your loss."

"Yes, thank you," she said. "And what are you doing here?"

"Something's wrong," Darren said. "She's usually sharp as a tack."

A growing sense of dread was taking hold of my stomach. Angie shouldn't have forgotten me in the short time since waking up on the couch. "I came to offer my condolences. Such a tragedy."

"All the times I told Darren to take care of himself, work less, exercise more..." She sighed heavily. "I can't believe that someone killed him."

Ben sat on the couch beside her and took his mother's hand. "I know it's quite a shock."

"All I want is to help." Since she hadn't answered my earlier question, I repeated it, "Can you tell me anyone who might have wanted to hurt your husband?"

She shook her head, then turned to her son. "When did you get here? I thought you were in your room."

My sense of unease grew even more.

Ben said, "Mom, I've been here since you fainted in the hall. I helped Emma carry you in here."

"Fainted? Don't be ridiculous." She turned to me. "Hello, dear. My name is Angie. Who are you?"

Oh, no.

That sinking feeling grew stronger.

"Mom? This is Emma," Ben said. "She told you that."

"I'm sorry, I don't remember. How did I get here?"

My heart pounded. This wasn't right. I did the spell to erase Angie's memory of me telling her about Darren's ghost. She was supposed to forget the sixty seconds before the spell happened. Instead, she was losing her short-term memory *every sixty seconds.*

TWELVE

A choking sound escaped me. Everything fell into place. The spell to make Angie forget my mention of seeing ghosts backfired. Instead of forgetting the last sixty seconds one time, the spell appeared to be resetting itself every minute. What happened?

The magical cloth wasn't supposed to erase her memory over and over. I should never have attempted such big magic so soon after using that eavesdropping spell. I was still pretty new, and I'd overextended.

What had I done? How did I make it right?

Darren realized what happened at the same time I did. "What did you do? Fix her!"

"I don't know." I shook my head and stepped backward, although, as a ghost, Darren couldn't hurt me. "This wasn't supposed to happen."

Ben's head shot up. "What wasn't supposed to happen? What did you do?"

"I should go," I said desperately.

Even if I knew how to undo the spell, the Magical Enforcement Office prohibited using magic in front of humans. Ben wouldn't leave me alone with his mother. I also couldn't do a spell and ask to erase his memory. Not that I wanted to try again and risk further disaster. Angie looked so thoroughly confused, it broke my heart. It was time to call for reinforcements.

"I'm calling the police," Ben said. He patted his pockets, then glanced upstairs and swore. "My phone is upstairs. Don't move."

Yeah, right. My eyes darted around frantically as he walked away. I could race out the front door, but Ben was between me and it.

The double patio doors stood about a dozen feet away from the living room sofa, letting in a great deal of light. Although I didn't know my way around their backyard, it seemed like a better means of escape than pushing Ben aside in the front hall.

Darren saw the direction of my gaze. "You're going to run away?"

"I can't fix this myself," I hissed. "If Ben calls the police, there's no way out of this. I need to go get help."

"What kind of help, dear?" Angie asked from the couch. "By the way, I don't think we've met."

"You promise you can fix her brain?" Darren asked.

"I hope so." Without waiting for further permission, I darted through the rear doors. As odd as it would appear to Angie, she wouldn't remember by the time Ben asked her where I'd gone.

The French doors swung open onto a gorgeous bricklined back porch, complete with color-coordinated flowering plants around the edges, an enormous outdoor kitchen, and a full living room set. Any other time, I'd have stopped to admire it. Instead, I pelted across the concrete, heading around toward the front of the house where I'd left my car.

As I ran, I fumbled around for my keys.

"What are you doing?" Darren said. "Run! Get out of here!"

"I need to unlock the car!"

He snorted, an admirable feat given how fast we were going, but ghosts didn't need to breathe. "Keyless entry, remember? Go! Go!"

Thank goodness for small favors. If we'd been racing out to my old Corolla and it refused to start, I'd have been in a heap of trouble. Instead, I threw open the door to my new SUV, dove inside, and stabbed at the ignition button. The engine purred to life. Not bothering to buckle my seat belt, I slammed the car into gear and stomped the accelerator at the same time the front door swung inward.

Ben appeared in the opening. With a shout, he raced toward me.

Darren turned toward the window and cackled. "Think you can outrun a Porsche, Sonny?"

It would have been funny if my heart hadn't been racing so fast. Or if I hadn't potentially caused irreparable harm to someone's brain. I gasped for breath.

We didn't drive far. After a couple of turns, Ben gave up the pursuit. I slowed down to the subdivision's ludicrously low speed limit.

"What are you doing?" Darren demanded. "Go! Security will be looking for us."

"I told you, we need help." My phone had automatically connected to the console when I started the engine, so I just needed to tap the screen a few times to make a call.

In theory.

Apparently, you're not allowed to scroll through your

Contacts app while driving. The electronics shamed me when I tried. But with Darren's help, I found the voice activation feature. "Call Dottie."

She picked up quickly. "Emma! How are you?"

"Um, not great," I said. "I need your help."

It occurred to me as the words left my mouth that I might be in less trouble from the police than if I admitted to my mentor that I'd done a memory wipe that backfired. She'd warned me about attempting advanced spells before I was ready. As a Magical Enforcement Office Witch, she could turn me into the Council for unauthorized use of magic.

Too late to worry about that now since Dottie was already asking, "What happened?"

"I told this woman that her dead husband spoke to me and she passed out so I did a spell to wipe the last minute from her memory and now she's forgetting everything every sixty seconds and I'm so sorry and oh, no, what have I done?" A sob escaped me.

"Where are you?" she asked.

I named the intersection ahead, and the line went dead. "Hello? Dottie?"

Barely had I finished her name when Dottie appeared in the passenger seat beside me. On top of my ghostly companion.

"What are you doing, lady?!" Darren yelled. He lunged forward, causing me to slam on the brakes.

Good thing we'd only been going eleven miles per hour.

"Goodness! What was that?" Dottie asked.

"How? Where? What?" The words sputtered out of me. Closing my eyes, I took a deep breath and tried again. "How did you do that? What are you doing here?"

"Well, that's a fine how-do-you-do. I came to save you."

"Could you please get off me?" Darren said.

I took a deep breath. "Let's start over. Hi, Dottie. It's nice to see you. Thank you for coming. I didn't realize you could travel that way."

"Oh, yeah. We don't do it much, but this was an emergency. Also, I did a time pause on the area. Which you should absolutely never do. That kind of magic is only allowed with council permission. I have it, you don't. Much like you don't have memory-wiping authorization."

"I really am very sorry," I said. "Let me take you back to the house while I explain."

"What about me?" Darren yelled.

"Sorry, Darren. Sit somewhere else." To Dottie, I said, "You teleported into a ghost. It was his wife we came to meet. He can move to the back."

Darren sputtered, but passed through the rear of the seat into the middle row. Goosebumps rippled down my arms.

With great care, I turned the car around and headed back. We didn't see any police cars. However, when I turned onto Darren's street, we spotted Ben. He stood as still as a statue, stopped in mid-stride. One foot was raised, and his mouth hung open as if he'd been yelling.

When I finally realized what happened, the enormity of Dottie's power hit me. "So when you said you paused time, you meant that literally."

"Of course. You think I'd make that up? I'm going to wipe everything from when you arrived. They shouldn't remember meeting you. I'll have to change the doorbell footage, too. It's better if you go. Don't contact them again."

I sighed. "I can't leave. We need to know who killed Angie's husband. Ben's stepfather. The ghost in the backseat."

She shook her head. "These spells are delicate, as you must have realized. You can come back tomorrow. That's non-negotiable. You promise, or I'll bring in the full council."

The set of her jaw told me not to argue. With a heavy heart, I parked in front of Darren's house.

"Do you need help getting Ben back inside?" I asked.

She shook her head. "No, I can manage on my own, thanks. Go. We'll talk later."

"Right. I'm sorry," I said. "I'll see you later."

"Wait!" She held out her hand. "Give me the memory mask."

My heart sank, but I shouldn't have been surprised. My malfunctioning spell could have been a disaster. Would have been, if Dottie hadn't saved me. It made sense she would confiscate it. Without making a fuss, I handed it over.

She examined the fabric, flipping it over. "This is pretty good. I think your downfall was the zigzag stitch. Her memory is going back and forth. But until I do a full analysis, don't make another one."

"Don't worry." This foray into memory magic had satisfied any urges for the next ten years or so. "I'm so drained, I couldn't make another one if I wanted."

Dottie exited the car, striding toward the front door without looking back. A moment after she crossed the threshold, Ben vanished from view down the street. Hopefully, Dottie had pulled him inside with her.

Darren took this all in without blinking. "You know weird people."

"Says the ghost."

"Being dead isn't my fault. I'm not changing time and appearing out of nowhere."

"Yeah, yeah." We didn't know how long Dottie would take. Given how she appeared, she wasn't likely to need a ride home. She might even be angry to find me waiting when she was done, since she'd directed me not to talk to Angie or Ben again today. "Let's go home."

"Home? When we don't know who killed me yet?"

"We can't stay here," I began.

"I heard that. Listen, we need to go to my office. Get some files."

"You want me to steal documents? I'd rather not get arrested by both the magical and human police in the same day."

"Then don't get caught," he retorted. "I thought you wanted to question my old assistant."

"I do. That should be our next stop."

"Her address is in my office."

I sighed. "Fine. How do we get in?"

"I'll give you the code for the alarm. Everyone should be gone. But there's other stuff that could tell you who killed me."

"What if I call the police with an anonymous tip? I'm not doing so great at this detective thing. Maybe I should hang up my metaphorical magnifying glass."

"You can call them, but I'm not going to stop badgering you and you can't walk away from me." He took a deep breath, as if to resume the singing from earlier.

My poor ears couldn't take the pain. "Okay, fine. What's the address?"

THIRTEEN

Darren's ad agency was about twenty minutes from his home. On the way, he explained that Angie's father originally owned the firm. When the relationship turned serious, Angie asked her father to give Darren a job as an entry-level advertising specialist. He did well, and when it was time to expand the business, Darren got promoted to partner.

"It wasn't this place, though. It was tiny. Marshall and I ran it together for a long time."

"How did you get along?"

He shrugged. "Okay. He had all the money, but I was pretty good at coming up with slogans. I learned how to prepare a pitch and started bringing in my own accounts, but for the first few years, he carried me. "

"That must have been rough. Does he still work there?"

"Nah. He left almost fifteen years ago." Darren crossed his arms. "When Marshall retired, he gave his share to Angie's brother. I protested, but nothing to do about it. It was Marshall's company; he could give it to William if he wanted. Now the two of us run the business together as partners."

"Were you upset?"

"Sure, but what could I do? I owe Marshall everything. My wife, my house, my job, everything. If he wanted to throw away his share by giving it to his son, who was I to argue?"

"Do you like your brother-in-law?"

"He's okay. William isn't a bad guy. He's great at schmoozing people. Doesn't have any business sense, though. Loyal as a Golden Retriever, and about as smart."

"So he manages the people and you handle the money?"

"Yeah. He's got no head for finance. I handle that stuff while he works on wooing the clients. The guy has buckets of charisma. We both create pitches, and overall, we work well together. There it is. Turn left."

The advertising agency rented space in a large building with several other businesses. Cars dotted the sprawling parking lot. He'd said his office would be closed, and I hoped he was right. I parked in an empty space marked for customers and took several deep breaths to prepare for breaking in.

The sun had already begun its descent, although we should have light for another hour. This day seemed endless. I'd arrived at the spa at eight o'clock this morning and it wasn't even dinnertime yet.

"Is there a security guard or cameras?"

"Nah. You walk in. There's a staircase to the left. We're up there."

"What's my reason for being here?"

"You shouldn't need one. We're closed."

"On a Wednesday?"

"Most of the staff probably went home when I died.

William would have given them permission. That's why they like him better."

"He's gone, right? Not likely to catch us inside."

"And you're sure he's in California?"

"Positive. Wasting time teaching others to succeed."

"Did you argue about that?" Never did I forget I was speaking with a ghost, trying to figure out who killed him.

"Nah. Like I said, the guy's a human Golden Retriever. Always happy, nice to everyone. Wouldn't know an argument if it bit him on the keister. Let's go."

He slid through the passenger door and floated up to the building. I watched him go, thinking about what a terrible idea this was. Anyone could see me walking into a closed office and call the police. Or an employee might be there unexpectedly. So many things could go wrong.

My ghost seemed undeterred by the risks.

At the door, Darren beckoned me. I closed my eyes, willing myself to find a way out of this. Three seconds later, Darren began to sing. Well, shout song lyrics.

My new car had many cool features, but, unfortunately, it wasn't soundproof.

With a heavy sigh, I opened my car door and followed him.

The outer door was unmanned, like Darren said. I followed him up the stairs and past several closed doors until I found one with his agency's name on it. An electronic keypad on the wall looked off until Darren told me to push the zero spot. It sprang to life. He gave me the code, and the door popped open.

"No key? I like it. But won't someone wonder why your code was being used after you died?"

He shrugged. "That's the default code."

"Let me guess—did Eve use that code to visit after hours?"

"None of your business."

While Darren led me to his office, I mulled that one over. He ran a company with his brother-in-law, using money originally gifted by his wife's father. They weren't close. He snuck his girlfriend onto the property after hours.

If William knew half as much about Darren's activities as I did, he'd be by far my most obvious suspect. Too bad he was in California. If he'd been attending a conference in New York City, Boston, or even Montreal, he might have snuck back and left again with no one realizing it. But unless he owned a private jet, California didn't work.

I had no idea how these people lived. "Did William take a corporate plane to the conference?"

"Nah, he flew commercial. I know what you're thinking. That guy's too dumb to kill me."

If only I shared Darren's confidence. Then again, he thought everyone was too stupid or incompetent to kill him. Someone had done it, so either Darren underestimated at least one person in his life, or he'd been killed by a total stranger.

Unlikely, but it wasn't beyond the realm of possibility. Officer Peterson thought I'd done it, and Darren was a stranger to me this morning.

This office had embraced the "open concept" look, turning a large room into a sea of cubicles. The far side had walls made entirely of glass. I understood the importance of being connected to the employees and letting in light, but it felt very exposed. When I saw Darren's full-length windows covered with blinds, I stopped. He floated right through me. So disconcerting, not feeling a thing.

"What are you doing?"

I gestured and lowered my voice. "We can't see through the blinds. What if someone is in there?"

"Who would invade my private space?" His booming voice made me wince, even knowing no one could hear it.

"I don't know—William returned early? Eve, covering up the evidence of your affair? Your stepson, looking to destroy a will that excludes him?"

There were plenty of cars parked in the lot. For all we knew, the entire cast of *Les Mis* might be in there.

"Just go in and tell me if it's empty."

"How will you know I'm not lying?"

Good question. "Because you need me."

Darren let out a heavy sigh. "You'd think they'd give me a medium with more of a sense of adventure."

"I'm not a medium. I'm a witch. Ghostly beggars can't be choosers."

Without replying, Darren floated through the wall. A moment later, he stuck his head out, leaving his body inside. "All clear."

Darren apparently didn't believe in locks, which surprised me. He seemed the sort to want to keep his secrets away from prying eyes.

"Do you have a cleaning crew after hours?" I asked.

"Every night at seven. You should be gone by then."

"Thanks for the heads up." The clock on the wall told me we had less than an hour. "Where do I find Casey's address?"

"On the computer. You'll have to log in."

"They're not printed anywhere?" Logging in meant touching the computer, which risked leaving fingerprints or, worse, hair. It also meant using a dead man's credentials, which would send up many red flags.

"Not since about 1990."

I glared at him. "Point taken."

He directed me to log in to his assistant's computer and showed me where to get the information. Since I didn't want to touch more than absolutely necessary, I snapped a picture on my phone. Then I started to log out.

"Wait. There's another thing we need."

"Why? You think we'll find evidence of motive here? Death threats, something like that?"

"Don't be stupid," Darren snapped. "There are files on my computer that I don't want William to find."

"Uh-uh." I shook my head. "No way. I'm not deleting files for you. If anyone finds out I was here, I can't possibly explain it. Getting the address is risky enough, but we didn't have a choice."

He huffed and acted like he wanted to scream again, but he must have seen my resolve. Everyone had lines they wouldn't cross, and I refused to go to jail for hacking and destroying evidence.

"You said we could find evidence here to tell us who killed you."

"Yeah, about that. I lied." He didn't look the slightest bit remorseful about it, either.

Before he could stop me, I logged out and wiped down the keys many times with a tissue from a box on the corner of his assistant's desk.

In an overabundance of caution, I put the chair back where I found it, wiped it down, and stuffed the used tissues in my pocket.

"Was that it? I'm ready to go."

"No," Darren said. "Pull out the top center drawer of my desk. Feel underneath—there's a key taped there. Got it? Good. Take it. Open the bottom right drawer. There's a lockbox under everything.

The drawer in question contained many things—file folders, blank finance documents and contracts, and several black account ledgers labeled from about 1998 onward. Then, finally, a gray rectangular lockbox at the bottom, almost as big as the drawer itself.

"Tell me you didn't bring me here to steal the petty cash," I said, although I pulled it out and put it on the desk. The thing must weigh at least five pounds. "I won't risk getting caught with this."

"You don't have to," he said. "When we're done, you'll put the box back. We want what's inside. I need you to follow my directions exactly and not ask questions."

I didn't like this. At Darren's direction, I opened the box. It contained a couple hundred dollars in cash and a stack of receipts, as expected. Then he told me to pull out a tray at the bottom.

Beneath it was a slim green book with "Account Ledger" stamped on the front. Maybe an old one? Pulling it out, I checked the year—but then I realized there was more underneath. Several more, dating back to 2017. I picked up the most recent one and flipped through it. Then I pulled out the non-hidden black ledger from the drawer and compared it.

"Stop that! Those are my private files!" Darren said.

"Then don't ask me to steal them for you." I flipped back and forth, confirming dozens of transactions that didn't match. Someone named Katherine was getting independent contractor pay in one book but not the other. One ledger showed a large severance payout to Barney, yet the other didn't. Our conversation left me pretty sure he'd never gotten the money. A bunch of smaller transactions didn't match up. With each new discrepancy, my heart sank further.

My initial instinct upon finding this secret second set of books was correct: Darren had been embezzling from his company. If his partner found out, this information gave William an excellent motive for murder.

I snapped several pictures with my phone before putting everything back, in case I wanted to review them on my own when I had more time. Other suspects might be hidden in the ledgers. Who was Katherine?

When I finished, everything went back into the metal box. I slammed it shut and jammed the key into the lock.

"What are you doing?" Darren shouted. "Take the books!"

"Absolutely not," I said. "These books are evidence. Let the police find them. As soon as we are far away, I'm making an anonymous tip."

"Stop. You can't do that. That's not why we're here."

"We're here to get an address, which we now have."

"That's why you're here. I have my own agenda."

"Oh, really? Enlighten me. Why are we here?" As soon as the words left my lips, I knew the answer. "You don't want your wife to find these. Why? It's too late for her to divorce you."

His cheeks turned red, and he averted his gaze. "Would you want to endanger someone you loved? If Angie sees the books, she'll want to know where the money went. She doesn't know I set up offshore accounts."

"You're putting money aside for Eve." I sighed heavily. "Is that what these payments to Katherine are? It looks like a lot of money."

"I plead the fifth."

"Fine, don't tell me. But I'm not helping you with this. Sing and shout in my ear all you want. I'm done. We're going home."

"Can we compromise? Put everything back. Toss the key in a dumpster outside so police can't open the box."

"Negative, Ghost Rider," I said in my best *Top Gun* impression. "I'm not tampering with any more evidence."

"Will you at least wait until tomorrow to call the cops?" he asked. "If they find this earlier, fine. If not, that gives us time to plan."

"I have a plan," I said. "Leave before we get caught. Tell the police about your cooked books. Inform them William killed you because you're stealing from him, and that the jury probably won't blame him. Watch you go into the light. I'm not going down as your co-conspirator."

FOURTEEN

Half an hour later, we finally turned into the mansion's sweeping driveway. It felt like I'd been away a million years, rather than hours. As always, the gorgeous old Victorian brought a smile to my face. When I'd arrived, the place had been in a total shamble. Immediately, I'd rolled up my sleeves and dedicated myself to fixing everything up.

Now, the place was absolutely stunning, from the wraparound porch to the massive windows and the new roof. The complete overhaul only took time, TLC, and a bit of magic.

Er... dedicated contractors.

"This is where you live?" Darren asked when we parked near the front porch. "After seeing your car, I expected a tent in the woods somewhere."

Without answering, I pushed the off button and exited the SUV. An off button! So cool. Darren slid through the passenger door and followed me toward the house.

When we passed my sign welcoming people to the bed-and-breakfast, he stopped, squinting and tilting his head.

"Emma's Home for Lost Souls. A bit of a mouthful, don't you think?"

"I wanted people to feel safe here."

"Then why don't you call it Haven?"

My mouth opened and closed as I resisted the urge to slap my forehead. "I didn't think of it. That's perfect."

"You're welcome. If I were alive, that would cost you five hundred bucks."

"If you were alive, I couldn't do this in front of you." With a touch to the sign, I transformed it. The letters rearranged to spell *Emma's Haven*.

He let out a low whistle. "Not bad."

"You don't want to mention the ghosts?" The question came from my front porch where my black cat waited. His former owner had named him Pink.

After the performer, not the color. After growing up with a dog named Bowie, I didn't judge, although I wished he would spell it with the exclamation point: P!nk.

"Good point." Another wave of my hand, and the sign flipped to reveal *Haunted Haven*. Then I said, "This one's just for the magical folk. Did Walter come back without me?"

"Excuse me?" Darren said loudly. "Are you ignoring me to talk to a cat?"

Pink drew himself upright. "I am not *just a cat*, sir. Emma, yes, he's in his old room."

"It's true," I said. "He's about a hundred years old, and he's magic. He's also much more snuggly than you."

Not waiting for a reply, I headed up the steps. Darren could follow or stay outside, whatever made him happy. Behind me, I heard a snort that could have been him or Pink.

In the kitchen, Josie was dribbling tiny bits of batter

onto the sizzling griddle. No one else was around. She smiled warmly when she spotted me. "My favorite guinea pig. Is everything okay?"

"No, things aren't okay!" Darren shouted. "I'm dead!"

For the moment, I ignored her question. "I need to find Walter. I took off my necklace at the spa without thinking and—poof!"

"Yeah, Pink spent about an hour in his old bedroom comforting him."

"You mean your room?"

"Why, yes. It *is* my room now. Funny you should mention that. Being able to hear only the meowed half of a conversation is rough. I've been here for hours, testing out new recipes. Which brings me to pancake buttons."

"Pancake buttons?" It felt like we were speaking different languages. Even Darren looked confused.

"Yeah. You know when you pour batter on the grill, there are always these tiny drips and drabs that cook instantly?"

"The last time I tried to make pancakes, the fire department showed up. Then three people accused me of poisoning my ex." That story was for another day.

"I knew it!" Darren shouted. "You killed me. All this 'investigating' was to throw me off your scent."

"Why would I do that? It's easier not to help," I said.

Josie nodded toward the air behind me. "Hi, Walter."

"Unfortunately, this isn't him. I picked up another ghost at the spa. Darren isn't tied to me the same way, but I need to ask Pink about this."

"You say that like I want to be here," Darren grumbled. "It's not my fault no one else can hear me."

Quickly, I explained to Josie what happened and my attempts to gather information on who killed Darren.

"Emma." Josie's voice held a touch of reproach. "Do you remember what happened last time you got involved in a murder investigation?"

I shuddered as a chill went down my spine. "Vividly. Unfortunately, I'm not sure I have a choice. Darren is here, and he's not going anywhere until I give him answers. Also, while Tim—Detective Pratt, I mean—seems to believe in my innocence, the fact remains that the masseuse found me standing next to Darren's body, searching his pockets. Officer Peterson considers me the prime suspect."

"It's Tim now, huh?" I shifted my gaze from her face to the pancakes, so Josie continued, "We'll come back to that one. Why were you searching a dead man's pockets?"

"I needed his phone to call the police. Dumb, I know. Next time I'll walk away."

"Let's hope there isn't a next time."

"You're not done with this time!" Darren reminded me, as if I could forget.

Whether or not I liked it, I was a part of this. After talking to his former employee and accidentally erasing his wife's memory, I couldn't walk away.

"No argument there," I said to Josie. My stomach growled, reminding me that the spa's promised lunch got canceled. I'd been driving around for hours with nothing to eat other than the cheese and crackers offered at Barney's car dealership.

That felt like a lifetime ago.

"Can I make you something? Pancake buttons?"

Make... hold on. Josie had cooking magic. My head shot up.

"How is your potion-making? Do you know how to create a truth serum?" If I could slip Eve a potion, she would tell me what happened. At a minimum, I'd be able to figure out how involved she was. Whether she was working with someone else, killed Darren herself, or the killer poisoned Darren earlier.

Josie shook her head. "Serums are difficult to get right. Then the subject has to ingest it. Would you drink something prepared by a person being investigated for murder?"

"I'm not really being investigated," I grumbled. "But I see your point. By now, everyone knows who I am. Maybe you could take her a potion?"

"Me?"

"Yeah! You're local. You know everyone. Maybe bake something into a condolence cake."

"I'm sorry, no. I can't take part in another murder investigation. Not after the last one. I'm here to live a quiet life."

Immediately, I felt terrible. The poor woman had gotten arrested the last time I played investigator. "Sorry, Josie. Absolutely, don't do that. I'll find another way. Maybe I can convince Darren's widow to trust me."

"Why don't you ask her husband? See what she's interested in and use that to start a conversation."

"She enjoys staying thin and being rich," Darren said behind me. "Also sitting on the board of various charities and throwing massive fundraisers where all the attention is on her."

I repeated it for Josie's benefit, then asked him, "Any events coming up?"

"There was one this morning. She's been talking about it for weeks."

This morning? I never got a chance to ask Angie where she was during the murder.

"What time?"

"I don't remember. I didn't go. But usually she went to the venue early. Talked about it throughout breakfast."

"If Angie was at a public fundraiser all morning, she couldn't have killed her husband," I said. "That should be easy enough to confirm, but I just lost my second-best suspect."

"Sorry, Emma." Josie turned back to the griddle and scooped a bunch of teeny pancake fragments up with a spatula before transferring them to a plate.

I'd never heard of this, but they looked delicious. Crisp, light, and most importantly, buttery.

Taking a handful of the buttons cooling on the plate, I popped them in my mouth. I'd been partially right. The bites were crunchy and light. They tasted like butter—and fear. Josie put her feelings into her food, but that wasn't always a blessing. She was still working on control.

With effort, I swallowed. "Pancake buttons, you say? Or panic buttons?"

"I was thinking about calling them 'little drops of happiness,'" Josie said. "Your expression does not support that."

"You should probably try again when you're in a better mood. The recipe is great, but the anxiety is not."

"Sorry. I was worried about you. Is everything okay?"

"Have you seen Toby this morning?" I asked.

While my next-door neighbor and I had our differences —he used to hate me—he was alone over there. Josie would make extra of whatever she was cooking for supper, or I would show up and tidy a bit. Sometimes one of us would stay and chat, share the local news. Little things to help. I felt obligated to check in on him when I could. Toby and Walter used to be good friends, and part of me felt like I owed it to my grandfather to take care of him. As Walter loved to point out, I never once visited while he was alive.

Toby acted like he didn't appreciate our efforts, but he'd

be sad if Josie and I stopped coming over. We were growing on him.

Josie grinned at my question. "Interestingly, no. I didn't have to."

"What do you mean?"

"T is over there. Toby used to be quite the gardener, you know. Gave it up a few years ago when he started to get arthritis."

"Yeah?"

"T is so excited about helping him out, he actually smiled."

"Wow."

T didn't talk about his personal life much, but he'd spent most of his senior year of high school couch-surfing with friends. The mansion was the first stable home he had known in a long time. He refused to talk about his parents and rarely answered personal questions. We didn't push— after all, Josie had her own secrets (not to mention my witchyness, ghost, and talking cat). He'd open up when he was ready.

I wasn't remotely motherly, so if T found a parental figure in my neighbor, I supported that one hundred percent. They might be good for each other.

Speaking of parental figures, it bothered me that Walter hadn't appeared since I returned from the spa. He must be pretty upset about what happened, and I didn't blame him. Even though it was an accident, I felt terrible for sending him back here. Time to apologize.

FIFTEEN

Since Josie said Pink was comforting Walter in her bedroom, I asked if she minded me going in without her.

"Do you know how confused I'd be if I went along? Listening to a three-way conversation with one human, a cat, and someone I can't hear? No, thanks. Just thinking about it is making my head spin." She made a shooing gesture. "See if you can cheer him up before my bedtime. I prefer to sleep alone."

Halfway across the lobby, I realized Darren had trailed along behind me. I hesitated. "This is a family matter. It might be better if you waited."

"Okay, sure," he said. "How are you going to stop me from following you?"

"Why do you want to come?"

"I don't have anything else to do." He grinned, a chilling smile. "Except practice my singing."

Ugh. I couldn't wait until this ghost moved on. At least he wasn't trying to force me to create ad campaigns anymore.

Josie's suite contained a bedroom, a sitting room, and a private bath. I found Walter sitting on the couch in her sitting area. Someone had turned on her TV, and he gazed blankly at it. Pink sat curled up beside him.

"Walter! I am so sorry about sending you back. I didn't know—"

Darren moved between us and looked back and forth. "Hold on. You never said you knew other ghosts."

"You didn't ask," I retorted. "And actually, yes, I did. Back at the spa, I told you we already have a ghost at the mansion. You weren't listening."

Walter stood. "And who is this? Did you send me away so you could canoodle with another spirit?"

I went to my grandfather, wishing for the hundredth time that hugging a ghost was possible. "No, of course not! I'm so sorry. I didn't think about the necklace. When you warned me, I didn't register what you were saying until it was too late. But look! I'm wearing the locket now. We can go anywhere you like."

"And by anywhere, you mean, to solve my murder?" Darren interrupted. "Do I have to wait in line behind Grandpa?"

"What are you doing here? Emma, you can't bring home any dead guy you meet on the street. It's my house, Sonny, so if I tell you to wait in line—"

"Stop!" My yell made both of them flinch. "Everyone, let's take a step back. Walter, you may remember Darren from the Relaxation Room. After you left the spa, he was murdered."

"Was that because he sat on someone else?" Walter muttered. "Yeah, I recognize him now. Jerk."

"We don't know why," I said as patiently as I could. "That's why he's here. We're working on it. Darren, this is my grandfather, Walter Sparrow. He lives in the mansion with me."

"You let ghosts stay here?"

"He's family."

Both of them started talking at once, speaking so fast I could barely follow. Pink sat on the couch, avidly moving his head from one to the other. A dull throbbing started behind my temples.

"Can you watch them?" I asked my cat. "It's been a long day, and I need a ghost break."

"They'll be fine," Pink said, jumping off the couch. "Did you bring me any treats?"

A chuckle escaped me. Naturally, that was his first concern. "T's been growing catnip in the garden. Go see how it's going."

After Pink trotted toward the kitchen, I backed out of the room, leaving the ghosts at each other's throats. They couldn't hurt each other, and I wasn't up for mediating. Too many other things were bothering me, like Officer Peterson accusing me of murder. If they found poison in Darren's teacup, she'd be happy to slap the cuffs on me. I couldn't deny touching it, and Walter couldn't testify as to my innocence.

Upstairs, I went to the antique wooden trunk at the foot of my king-sized bed. This piece belonged to my grandfather, and it had been warded so only his heir could open it. The entire third-floor suite was layered with similar protections. No one should climb the stairs to my rooms, and if they did, the doorway made people forget their destination when they passed through, unless I was with them. Any trespassers should immediately get a compelling urge to look for me downstairs. This house was a haven, and my rooms provided a personal sanctuary.

In case someone got past those protections, I'd added a layer of my own to the trunk. We didn't know how long Walter's spells would last after his death.

Opening the trunk, I pulled out my grandfather's heavy old spell book. Only magic preserved the crumbling paper. A lot of power lay in these pages, waiting for me to unlock it.

In contrast, I'd put my new spells in a Lisa Frank notebook. When I found the bright pattern at a local superstore, I'd been ecstatic to revisit my childhood. Pink said he needed sunglasses to look at it, but I loved the vibrant colors. Ninety percent of the pages were blank, but Dottie would fill up as I learned and grew more confident. At the moment, my book didn't carry one tenth of the power of Walter's.

I flipped through my grandfather's grimoire. Did Walter have a truth spell? Something to make people confess? Last month, I called up a vision of the past to view a murder. Unfortunately, I sincerely doubted Suzanne would let me waltz into the crime scene with a bag of ingredients and start lighting candles.

Mostly, Walter's powers were the same as mine. He was good with clothes and thread, which lent itself to general cleaning magic. Walter had a spell for growing tomatoes, but no murder-detection or truth spells.

Or at least, not ones that his book was ready to tell me about. That way lay a dead end.

My restless feet carried me down the stairs to the laundry alcove on the second floor. Since my wardrobe rejected stains and wrinkles, it wasn't a place I visited often. But I couldn't exactly offer a witchy laundry service to everyone, so the machines remained available for guests.

Missy was in the spa's laundry room folding linens

when the murder happened. A spa required a significant amount of cleaning, sterilizing, and disinfecting. Could that explain the smell I'd picked up? Something as mundane as clean bedding on the massage table? It might be entirely unrelated to the murder. But I had no other leads, so I might as well narrow it down.

In the cupboard over the front-loading washer and dryer, I found a stack of dryer sheets. Pulling one out, I lifted it to my nose and inhaled deeply.

Yuck.

"Spring fresh," my foot. It contained a faint chemical odor, though, which suggested I could be on the right track. It wasn't what I'd smelled in Eve's room, but not that different.

After tossing the sheet in the trash, I reached for the bottle of detergent and unscrewed the cap. This smelled better than the fabric softener, but still not the scent I wanted.

"Did someone tell you all the cool kids are huffing laundry soap these days?" T's voice from the doorway almost made me drop the bottle. He held a towering basket of dirty clothes in front of him. "Because we've talked about you trying to be cool."

"Hilarious." I turned to my youngest resident with a smile. "How are you? Everything okay at Toby's?"

"Fine. I'm teaching him how to write code for his website."

When I met Toby, he was a grumpy seventy-two-year-old man who touched computers as little as possible. The thought of him learning to code made me smile. But the important thing was that T had connected with my neighbor.

"I thought he was teaching you to garden."

"We're helping each other," he said. "Besides, I already know plants."

"Toby's been gardening twice as long as you've been alive. You might learn a thing or two."

"Either way, it's nice to hang out in the sun and play in the dirt." He moved around me and started putting clothes into the front of the washing machine. If he'd noticed that I hadn't explained why he'd caught me sniffing detergent, he didn't care. "Who's the new guest?"

"New guest?" I shook my head. "Did you see someone downstairs? I should go check them in."

"Nah, there's a Porsche in the driveway. Don't tell me you didn't see that big ol' SUV. It is on fire! Brand-new, all-wheel drive, goes up to 177 miles per hour, 541 horses in that baby. From 0 to 60 in under four seconds. It's 6,400 pounds of premium automotive engineering. Aw, man, I'm drooling. I can't wait to meet the owner. Hey, do you think they'll let me take it for a test drive?"

I chuckled. "Oh, sorry. I forgot to tell you—I got a new car today."

"Yeah, right. It's not April Fool's Day."

"I'm serious! It's a long story."

"Did it involve your old car exploding in a towering inferno?"

"Hey! If you want to drive the Porsche, don't talk about my girl like that. I'm going to miss her."

He was practically drooling. "I would say anything right now if it meant driving that beauty. Will you marry me?"

"No. But I could use your help."

"Who is it, and where do you want the body buried?"

I snorted. "You better not make that offer to anyone who'll think you're serious. When I was at the spa earlier, someone died."

"What? For real?"

"A man died on his table. It was awful. I'm trying to figure out what happened."

"Maybe he had a stroke."

"The police don't think so. His lips were green, like he'd been poisoned. There was no blood, bruising, or signs of a struggle."

"Why do you care?"

Because the man's ghost is loud and obnoxious and following me around? No, that wasn't it. Because I cared about helping people? Sort of. I went with the answer least likely to make him think I was crazy.

"I'm the one who found him."

"Yikes. You okay?"

"I think so, but someone else spotted me in the room. She thinks I'm guilty, and so does at least one police officer. I'm trying to find the cause of death, to narrow down the culprit. My best guess is poison. They use a lot of aromatherapy, and it's got me thinking. Is there a plant that might knock someone out if they breathed it in? Like an all-natural chloroform. What if the massage therapist put something in the diffuser?"

"A lot of poisons are transmitted by air."

"Any reasonably easy to get?"

He thought for a minute. "Opium? It comes from poppies. It's not native to New York, but you could get it. Especially with the City so close. You can get almost anything in New York City, from aspirin to napalm."

When he said "poppies," I pictured the Wicked Witch of the West putting Dorothy and her friends to sleep. Definitely a possibility.

"Would opium kill a person?"

"You would need a lot. And it's indiscriminate. Everyone would be knocked out."

The air in Eve's room seemed fine—an odd smell, but nothing that made me drowsy. Eve and Suzanne were unaffected, and Eve was in there the longest.

So much for that idea.

"Can you think of a natural poison that takes about half an hour to kick in? The guy was drinking tea before his appointment."

"There are a lot of possibilities. On TV, people drink poison and clutch their throats immediately, but it doesn't have to happen like that. It could be something harmless as long as you don't ingest it. He could have had an allergic reaction. Or he could have been poisoned slowly over time."

"What happens if I ingested a toxin that doesn't kill me right away? How would I feel?"

"Depends on what it is." He shrugged. "Once symptoms begin, you could be looking at nausea, dizziness, vomiting, fatigue, overall muscle weakness."

"Could a poison make your face go numb?" Darren mentioned feeling odd before the massage started.

"I'm sure something does. If you had a specific plant in mind, I could tell you more."

"Thanks, T. See you at dinner." On the way out, a thought occurred to me. T was studying for his G.E.D. and planned to take college courses online next semester. Eventually, he hoped to attend in person, but he only owned a bicycle. "My Corolla is at the dealership. Later this week, if you're not busy, will you go with me to pick it up?"

"You didn't trade it in?" Before I could answer, he shook his head. "Of course not. They wouldn't want it."

"But you do, right? Because if you come with me to get it, it's yours. I know it's not much—"

"Yes! It's the great car of all time! Thank you, thank you, thank you!" He stopped, and his face fell. "Hold up. I can't pay you for it."

My young friend didn't like charity, despite not having much. "You know me better than that, T. As long as you help around the mansion, it's yours. Do well in school, get your degree, and then buy me dinner. Better yet, pay it forward," I said. "Besides, you hate that car. When winter comes, you won't be thanking me at all."

"Any car beats a bicycle in the winter. I'll treat her well, I swear. Thank you."

AN HOUR LATER, I was resisting the urge to beat my head against my keyboard. T was right: Darren could have been killed by any of a dozen poisons. Grown locally, imported, made in a bathtub... the possibilities were endless. We couldn't narrow it down until the lab in Saratoga returned the test results, unless they found something at the crime scene.

Walking around and smelling random things was a waste of my time. I even did a Google search for "What does chloroform smell like?" but that told me nothing. This chemical scent wild goose had been chased enough.

My eyes were growing heavy from fatigue, and the now-dried oil in my scalp itched. When I'd rinsed off quickly at the spa, inches from Officer Peterson, I hadn't gotten as clean as circumstances warranted. Tomorrow, we needed to go back to the spa to question Eve, Suzanne, and Missy again. Today, it was time for a break.

Normally a long shower helped me think, but this time,

the gentle thrumming of the hot water did nothing to relieve the tension in my shoulders. Officer Peterson thought I might be involved in another murder. She could make my life difficult, even if Tim didn't consider me a suspect.

When I returned to my bedroom, both ghosts lounged on my bed. "What are you doing here?"

"Waiting for you, of course," Darren said.

I headed for the rear of my walk-in closet, away from ghostly eyes. "Why don't you go explore the property?"

"I'm not an outdoors guy," Darren said. "More of an action fellow. If you won't help me with my agency, we need to find out who killed me. Maybe you're right and William wanted to steal my share of the business."

I stepped into my favorite cotton pajama shorts and pulled a matching shirt over my head. Both these pieces were made by me, while thinking soothing thoughts, and they were the best anti-insomnia remedy I'd ever experienced. Instantly, I felt calmer than at any moment since finding Darren's body. Josie swore I'd make a killing selling them online, but I was content to make her a set for Christmas.

"I'm working on it. All day, we've been working on it, remember?"

"You're not closer than you were when I died."

"Hey, this isn't on me," I said. "You were in the room and still don't know what happened. I've got a list of suspects, at least two motives, and some ideas about a slow-acting poison."

"What?"

"Earlier, you said your lips grew numb on the way to the massage room. It's hard to believe that someone snuck in and killed you during the window between when Eve left and I showed up. I didn't pass anyone in the hall, and no one else was there when I arrived. Which probably means they used poison. One that would let you walk around for a bit before taking effect. You didn't see any poppies anywhere, did you?" It was a long shot, but it was what I had.

"What? You think I'm the kind of guy who stops to smell flowers? I wouldn't know a poppy if it bit me. I wanted to see Eve." He avoided my eyes. "Now that you mention it, I was having trouble focusing. Thought I was tired. Especially because I fell asleep after she left."

The fact that he died a few minutes later didn't make me feel better about Eve.

"Did you have anything for breakfast? What did you do this morning? Take me through your day."

"Got up at six o'clock, made coffee. While it brewed, Angie made me bacon and eggs, like usual."

"Did you see her make them? Did she use brown sugar?" Opium seemed less and less likely, but it didn't hurt to ask.

"Promise me you won't make eggs for anyone else." He shrugged. "I was reading my messages. But she ate everything, too."

Unless Angie had built up a tolerance to whatever incapacitated her husband, that was a dead end. She couldn't have given him a drug to knock him out hours later without also feeling the effects. "Then what?"

"Then her deadbeat son came in and started asking her for money. I left so he wouldn't hit me up, too. Got to the office before seven, where I worked on paperwork until we opened."

"You were cooking the books?" I asked.

Walter laughed. "I knew it!"

"Like you're so squeaky clean, Gramps," Darren said. "There were rumors about you, you know."

He puffed out his chest. "I got my money the old-fashioned way. Inherited every penny, then invested it. Not that different from you."

"I'm a self-made man!" Darren yelled.

Walter snorted. "Self-made with your wife's money! At least I admit it."

"Anyway," I interrupted loudly. "Did you see anyone at work? A parking lot altercation, anything? What happened next?"

"Everyone's due in the office by eight. Since William's out of town, I did the morning meeting with the sales guys, approved a couple of presentations, answered a lot of email. Then I left for the spa."

I thought back to our brief meeting. "You drank tea at the spa, right?"

"Tried to. Normally I like the tea there, but this stuff tasted awful. Completely bitter."

"Was anyone else around?" My first cup of tea had been fine. I decided not to drink my refill because of Darren's comment, but what if the fresh pot wasn't the problem? Anyone could have walked by and dropped something into his tea. "Did you leave your tea unattended at any point?"

"There were dozens of people. I left my tea on the table when I went to the bathroom, then found a lounger. Where, I might add, you moved the cup. Maybe you poisoned it."

Not this again.

"For the fiftieth time, I didn't kill you. If I had, I would exorcise you rather than helping."

The rooms were dark. A lot of people walked around. Most women my age knew better than to leave drinks unattended, but a big guy like Darren probably didn't think twice about it.

Suzanne didn't like him. She wouldn't like what he and Eve were doing in one of his rooms. Had she found out? Maybe she'd taken matters into her own hands: lure Eve out of the room by emptying her massage oil, kill Darren, then frame the masseuse for it. After all, Eve had the best opportunity. She also didn't have an alibi—no one confirmed seeing her after she led Darren from the Relaxation Room.

Although it seemed ludicrous that Suzanne would murder someone in her own business, maybe that was the genius of her plan. Everyone would assume she hadn't done it for the same reasons I did originally.

Smothering a yawn, I turned to the clock. It was much too late to follow up with Suzanne tonight. Everyone at the spa would be gone. I didn't have phone numbers for any of the staff, so I couldn't question them about their boss without going to the premises. Suzanne wouldn't let me in without an appointment, either. Unless I wanted to stand in the parking lot questioning employees as they arrived, I'd have to buy another day pass. The police wouldn't have forensic results yet, nor were they likely to tell me if they did. Walter would be thrilled.

There was nothing else for me to do but turn out the lights. Like it or not, this investigation would have to wait until morning.

SIXTEEN

The next morning when I woke up, Walter was sulking at the foot of my bed. He didn't appreciate having to share his space with another ghost. He insisted we remove Darren from the property immediately. No problem—except I couldn't. My hazy understanding of my ghostly power was that each individual would move on once I had helped them resolve whatever kept them in our world.

We had a long list of suspects and the knowledge that my newest ghost had been embezzling from the company he ran with his brother-in-law. Part of me still wanted to turn his books over to the police. With my luck, though, Darren would haunt me forever as revenge. Better to leave it alone and hope the police figured it out on their own.

Or an anonymous tip after he went through his door. The idea of him embezzling from the family that set him up financially didn't sit right with me. Sure, I'd inherited my wealth, but I didn't steal it. Walter left it to me willingly. If another heir showed up, like my mom, I'd share. If she ever put in an appearance, I would happily give her part of everything Walter left me. That was less likely than me finding a killer, though. We hadn't spoken in more than thirty years.

Although I wanted to return to the day spa, now that the dust of my botched memory spell had settled, it was time to talk to Darren's family. Keeping in mind what Darren had said about people taking me more seriously if I presented myself well, I eschewed my usual cozy yoga pants for a pair of black wool slacks and my favorite green cashmere sweater. Not exactly dressed for a night at the opera, but comfortable and presentable. Also perfectly fitted to me, which somehow made clothes look more expensive.

When Angie answered the door, her expression was as devoid of recognition as yesterday. "May I help you?"

No idea what happened yesterday. Internally, I heaved a sigh of relief.

Beside me, Darren grunted. "That's some pretty useful magic there, if you ever figure out how to use it correctly."

"Hi, Mrs. Cartwright. My name is Emma. I knew Darren. I'm here to offer my deepest condolences on your loss."

Her eyes narrowed. "How did you know my husband?"

Too late, I remembered that yesterday, she immediately jumped to the conclusion of us having an affair. My mind raced for a reasonable response, and I cursed myself for not inventing a story in the car. "He approached me about donating to one of your charities. I can't quite remember the name." That second line was said loudly and in Darren's direction.

He shrugged. "There are a ton. I can't keep them all straight."

Of course, he couldn't make this easier for me. Might as

well make something up. "I'm a seamstress. He was saying something about providing clothes for homeless women to go on job interviews. I can tailor anything you like."

Her face lit up. "Really? That's wonderful! Come in, come in."

As she led me into the living room, Angie told me she hadn't thought her husband listened when she talked about the various places she donated her time and energy.

"I didn't," he said. "That was one lucky guess."

With a side-eye at him, I said loudly, "It's a wonderful cause. I worked with a similar group back in college."

"Oh, really? Where was that?"

"A small town in Ohio; you probably haven't heard of it. Let me give you my card."

She took the small rectangle and eyed it as warily as if I'd offered her a handful of mud. Considering that it didn't identify me as a seamstress or philanthropist, I understood. In explanation, I said, "I inherited a bed-and-breakfast recently. But the number and email are current."

Her eyes narrowed. "Is that how you know my husband? Did he bring women to your establishment?"

"No, ma'am. We met at the spa yesterday. Darren was talking about how charitable you are."

"Took him long enough."

"Excuse me?"

"To appreciate me. He was seeing someone else," she said softly.

"I'm sorry to hear that."

She looked me square in the eye. "You don't seem surprised."

"Um, one of the spa attendants warned me he might have a wandering eye. How did you know?"

"I'm not stupid," she said. "Late nights at the office,

long after my brother had gone home. Credit card charges for meals I didn't eat, flowers never delivered. Last month, I stopped by his office one day to surprise him. Found a gorgeous diamond tennis bracelet in his top desk drawer. I was so pleased—it was a week before our anniversary, and I thought he'd forgotten."

"What happened?"

"He never gave it to me. Let our anniversary pass without mentioning it. The next time I visited him at work, it was gone. That's when I knew for sure."

Darren watched this revelation with his mouth open.

To Angie, I said, "That must have been difficult. I'm sorry."

She laughed bitterly. "You want to hear something ridiculous? I went to confront her. I was sure it was his assistant. Even when he fired her, I knew he only did it to get me to stop harassing him. So I tracked her down. She laughed in my face, said Darren was the last man she'd get involved with."

"The last?" Darren said. "That hurts."

"And you believed her?" I asked.

"I did. Her reaction was genuine. I still knew he was seeing someone, but you can't fake that level of surprise." She sighed.

If Angie didn't know Eve's name, I saw no reason to enlighten her. "The entire situation must have been very upsetting."

"He would have come around. He always did. Darren knew I would take care of him. He owed me everything."

"Did you ever think about leaving him?" I asked, mostly out of curiosity.

"Of course not." She gestured around her. "Look at all this! I have everything I want in life. We make a beautiful couple. As long as he was discrete, I wasn't worried about her. Even though, apparently, he should have been."

Her words made my ears perk up. "Do you have any reason to believe his mistress killed him?"

"Last week, I went through Darren's phone. That's when I found the texts with some massage therapist." As her husband shrieked in outrage behind me, I forced myself to keep my eyes trained on her face. "She thought he was going to leave me for her. That never would have happened. If she'd found out the truth, she might have killed him."

Eve seemed truly upset at his loss, but didn't know her at all. My natural inclination was to believe people were telling the truth until I received evidence to the contrary. All those "innocent until proven guilty" speeches on *Law & Order* over the years sank in. That made it more difficult for me to leap on Angie's assumption that Eve killed her husband, but I'd always known she had the opportunity. Now she also had a motive.

Footsteps on the stairs pulled our attention to the entryway. Darn it, she might have been about to tell me more. When Ben entered, Angie introduced us.

I acted like I'd never seen him before. "Nice to meet you. I'm sorry for your loss."

"Sorry, Mom. I don't mean to interrupt," he said. "I came down to see how you're doing."

"Everything will be okay. I must have slept twelve hours yesterday. Rest is remarkably healing."

Guilt made my cheeks grow warm. Dottie's spell knocked them out for half the day, and it was my fault.

"Still, don't overdo it," Ben said. "People are going to offer condolences."

"Yes, yes, I know. Emma is one of those people. She was

at the spa yesterday. Tell me, did you see Eve? Is she pretty? Was she wearing my tennis bracelet?"

"Gorgeous," Darren said from behind me. I'd almost forgotten he was there. "Her pure soul and inner beauty shine through."

Before I could say anything, Ben interjected. "Come on, Mom. That won't help."

"Don't I have a right to meet his little distraction?"

The conversation had taken a delicate turn. I didn't want to upset Darren's wife or get tossed out by Ben a second time. But maybe I could get more information before leaving.

"So you knew he was cheating, and you weren't happy about it. Yet you seem awfully secure in your marriage. You said she was upset that he wanted to stay with you. Are you positive he wouldn't have left?"

"I wanted out, you old bat!" Darren shook his fist under Angie's nose. She flinched, ever so slightly, and I wondered if it was a coincidence or if she actually felt his presence. He had said she was open-minded. Maybe she was in tune with the world around her.

Or maybe his emotions were powerful enough to create a breeze. If so, that was very interesting.

Angie smiled thinly. "We had an ironclad prenuptial agreement. When we got married, I brought quite a bit of money into the relationship. My father financed the entire agency. If Darren cheated, I'd get the house, the car, our vacation home, everything. My brother owns half the business now, and my husband's share would go to me. The employees never would have followed Darren to a new company. He would have been forced to resume his lifestyle from before we met. He would have died before letting that happen."

"Don't be so dramatic, Mom," Ben said. "He would have been fine."

"Fine, yet broke."

There was one more thing I needed to know. Darren had hinted at her having a solid alibi, but I hadn't checked it yet. Besides, I wanted to watch her reaction when I asked the question.

"Where were you yesterday morning?"

Ben drew himself up to his full height and glared at me. "And with that insinuation, I have to ask you to leave."

"Nice subtlety," Darren said. "You could learn a lot from working in sales."

"I'm so sorry," I said, although I wasn't. "I didn't mean to imply—"

"You did, too," Darren said. "Own it."

"It's fine, Benny," Angie said. "Everyone looks at the spouse when someone dies unexpectedly. I understand completely. My whereabouts are no secret. Yesterday morning, I hosted a fundraiser brunch for the children's hospital at the local zoo. Dozens of people saw me. Including my son, who could tell you as much if he weren't busy acting so offended."

At that, Ben looked away sheepishly. "Yeah, I was there. We both were. She ran the event, and I worked the bar."

"So sorry again. I look forward to working with you, Angie." Ben ushered me through the foyer as I spoke, and the last word wound up directed at the pane of glass on the front door.

Smooth.

"An ironclad alibi," I muttered while we walked to the car. Yes, I needed verify, but Darren had already told me the same thing. "Both of them."

Darren floated through the door and continued toward my car. "Come on. Are you going to talk to yourself all day?"

"That's what most people think I do."

All the way back to the mansion, Angie's words rang in my head. If Darren divorced her, he'd lose everything. He'd mentioned that he joined and helped expand his father-in-law's business, but not the rest of it.

Did Eve expect him to leave his wife for her? Or did she kill him in a fit of rage after learning he would never belong to her alone? They obviously really cared about each other. If they had different expectations for the future, that could have set Eve off.

She could have dropped poison in the teacup before Darren finished it. He'd said the drink tasted weird. By the time the police arrived, his cup would have taken to the kitchen and washed, destroying any evidence. The perfect crime.

Eve wasn't the sole possibility. Several people had motive: the betrayed wife, the business partner getting fleeced, the employee let go for wanting work/life balance, the illegally fired assistant, even the spa owner whose livelihood would have been threatened if word got out about Darren and Eve's relationship. Motive alone wasn't enough. Who had the opportunity to slip him the poison?

William was out of town. If Angie and Ben were at the fundraiser, they were out, too. I hadn't spotted either of them at the spa, anyway, and surely if they'd been there, the security footage would have picked them up. Same with Barney. I'd ask Tim to check the tapes for them, but I'd be shocked if anything came up.

Suzanne was there, Missy was there, and Eve was there. Of the three, only Eve seemed like a viable suspect. Suzanne's profitable business could be ruined by something like this. Missy's motive was weak. Sure, Darren was rude, but he wasn't the only unpleasant customer. She rarely had to deal with him, so why risk everything?

I tried to imagine how I would feel about a married man seducing me with false promises of wealth. The married man who seduced me as a twenty-something only promised an experience that turned out to be unsatisfying. But Darren and Eve had started a relationship. If she expected the affair to lead to a life together, how would she feel when that promise slipped away?

Who would have told her? Darren said he intended to stay with Angie. The texts Angie found confirmed that Eve thought they were going to be together. Darren didn't seem the type to accidentally reveal something that important. I'd believe Angie smirkingly informed Eve that her relationship was a dead end if Eve were the one who turned up dead. But maybe someone else let something slip—a business associate or mutual friend? Who would know the details? And when someone was conducting a secret affair, did they introduce her to their friends?

Maybe it was simpler than that, and Eve saw Darren with his wife somewhere.

"Did you and Angie have a romantic dinner out recently?"

He shrugged. "We went to a show in Saratoga a few weeks ago. Got dinner before."

"Did Eve know about it?"

"She knew Angie and I spent time together. I told her I had to act normal until my lawyer served the divorce papers."

How else could she have found out? Having never signed a prenuptial agreement, I didn't know who would be privy to the details.

"Who drafted your prenup?" I asked.

"Peter Watts," he said promptly. "If you want to protect your assets, you couldn't do better."

"Then why did your wife say you'd get nothing in a divorce?"

"She was the one who hired him. I was young and stupid back then. Let my parents talk me into using my cousin. Never work with family."

"Do you know where Peter is now?"

"He died about ten years ago. Heart attack. Hey, can we find him in the afterlife? I couldn't punch him in the nose before, but now I can! What do you think?"

Lovely. Now Darren wanted to start a ghost fight club. "Sorry, I don't know how to call specific ghosts. If he died that long ago, he's probably moved on. Most people do."

Darren snorted and turned toward the window. "Fine. Don't let me have any fun."

The lawyer couldn't have spoken with anyone. Unless Eve found a copy of the document, only Angie or Darren could have shared the information with her.

"Did Eve know about the prenup?"

"No, I was trying to get around it."

"You mean the money you've been embezzling?"

He didn't answer, which I took as confirmation.

"Did Eve know any of your friends and family? Any coworkers use the spa?" I asked. "Did your wife go there?"

"No way. Angie went to an overpriced 'luxury retreat' in Saratoga."

"Okay, maybe she found the prenup. Do you have a copy somewhere? In your office, anything like that?"

"Do I look dumb to you?"

I gazed at him pointedly, as if mulling over the question. Finally, I said, "You look translucent."

He snorted. "You're not as a funny as you think you are."

"I am exactly as funny as I think I am," I said. "Possibly not as funny as you think I want to be."

"Don't quit your day job. Anyway, there are two copies. One in a safe deposit box, which I can't get you into. The other is digital. I could give you the login for the account where I store everything, but there's no point. Everything Angie said is true. If I divorce her, that's it. I get nothing."

"What about the money you've been hiding?"

"Angie doesn't know that, and you're not going to tell her."

Even if I wanted to, I wouldn't say a word. "Did anyone else have access to your cloud account?"

"Just my lawyer. He set it up."

"Did you have your passwords written down?"

"No! I saved the login information on my computer. And my phone."

Anyone with access to his devices might have found the bank accounts, if they knew where to look. And Eve was in the massage room with Darren's phone before he died.

SEVENTEEN

When we arrived back at the mansion, I settled behind the front desk to do some digging on the B&B's computer. The Children's Hospital held a fundraiser yesterday morning at the local zoo, like Angie said. Ben and Angie appeared in multiple photos on social media, both before and after Darren's death. Angie looked like the emcee—She was in about a hundred videos and pictures. Not only would someone have noticed if she'd left, she would have been gone at least an hour. Angie didn't sneak into the spa and kill her husband.

No unusual results appeared when I searched for the ad agency. With Darren's help, I found a page for William's conference. He'd been tagged in more than a dozen posts, including pictures. It had been a long shot, anyway. Next up: Barney. Turned out, his accounts were full of pictures of him and his kids. He helped coach his son's Little League team. After meeting Barney, I'd never wanted to consider him a suspect. When I saw that he'd taken his daughter's preschool class on a field trip yesterday morning, I happily crossed him off the list.

The assistant who'd been fired didn't have any search-able accounts, but I still planned to talk to her. Darren didn't know if she'd gone back to school as planned or if she was working at a new job. Since I couldn't find any information online, we'd have to drop by her house and hope she was willing to talk to me.

I searched for Eve, but her social media profiles were locked down. Probably so she could post about her married boyfriend. Missy's posts were all pretty run-of-the-mill. Suzanne's personal pages were locked down, too. She posted a lot on the spa's accounts, which was to be expected. No leads on any of them, which was frustrating.

Shortly after lunch, to my surprise, the front door opened, and Ben appeared. Part of me expected him to spin around and walk away when he saw me, as if he'd come here by mistake. Instead, he grinned sheepishly.

"What brings you in?" I asked, hoping to sound friendly.

"Probably needs somewhere to lounge around, the worthless lout," Darren said behind me. "Trying to mooch some free cookies."

I held up one hand to Ben and turned my head so he wouldn't see I wasn't wearing a Bluetooth. Note to self: if ghosts keep popping up, pretend to be constantly on the phone.

"That's not very nice," I said to Darren.

"Neither is he. Just you wait. Wanted to take my money and blow it. Ungrateful—"

"Sorry to cut you off, but I've got a customer," I shouted. "I'll call you back."

As Ben approached the desk, I mimed removing an earpiece and stowing it under the desk. "Good morning! Welcome to Haven."

"Letting him in after I gave you a better name for your establishment," Darren grumbled behind me. "This is the thanks I get?"

Ben said, "Hey. I wanted to apologize for the way I treated you earlier. It was inexcusably rude."

"Thank you, but that's not necessary," I said. "Your stepfather died. You get a little slack."

"Thanks. We weren't close." He took a deep breath. "Anyway, I do have to apologize because I need a room."

"Oh, yeah? What happened?"

A sheepish smile crossed his face. "Nana showed up."

"You don't like your grandmother?"

"Oh, no. She's great. We get along fabulously. Probably my favorite family member. She and my mother, on the other hand..." He shuddered. "They bicker constantly. Nana always says grandkids and grandparents get along so well because we have a common enemy."

I grinned at him. "Sounds like something my Grandma Vera would have said."

"I'm not saying it isn't true, but they're both to blame here. Neither realizes they're putting me in the middle. Silly spats no one can win. It feels like I have to take Mom's side, even when she's wrong. Better not to be there."

"Yikes. I'm sorry." Since he seemed forthcoming with information, I probed a little deeper. "Your mom married Darren twenty years ago, is that right?"

"Yeah. My dad died when I was a kid."

"I'm sorry to hear that." I started to tell him I'd never known my father, but didn't want to get sidetracked. There was still a killer to find. Even with his solid alibi, anything Ben spilled about Darren might help.

"Me, too." He shook his head. "But enough of my sad

story. I hear you have nice, clean rooms, and the breakfast is amazing."

"Clean," Darren muttered under his breath. "What do you care? You haven't picked up the clothes off your floor in fifteen years."

Seriously, I needed to ask Dottie if she knew a ghost-muting spell.

Ignoring him, I smiled at Ben. "You're not from around here?"

"No. Well, yes."

"That clears it up."

He blushed. "Sorry. I mean, I grew up around here, but I moved to New York City after high school."

"New York is great. Did you go to school there?"

"Guilty. Got a degree in business to make Darren like me. I should've known nothing would work at that point. The man had a lump of coal where his heart should be." He smiled sadly. "Mom and I were happy before they got married. I mean, from my perspective. Things were better when it was the two of us. Sure, she was lonely, but she was nice. We were best friends. I know we're not supposed to speak ill of the dead, but..."

Especially not when they could hear you.

His words put me on high alert. Ben did not like his stepfather. Ben was not sad that Darren died. It would be incredibly short-sighted of me not to even consider the possibility that Ben was involved. Why did a morning fundraiser need a bartender, anyway? He could have snuck out and come back without anyone realizing it.

I'd been fooled once by a handsome face, and I didn't intend to be taken in again. As soon as he left, I'd send Tim a picture and ask him to check the video footage from the spa.

But if Ben were innocent, it would be unkind to turn him away. Indecision made me freeze in place, unable to go through the check-in process or even continue the conversation. If only Darren could tell me if Ben had killed him. Considering their relationship, he would've been happy to share.

Meanwhile, I'd strengthen the protective spells on this place and ask Pink to keep an eye on Ben. Maybe Dottie knew an "anti-violence" spell for the entire building. Until then, I had some tricks up my sleeve.

Ben's eyes met mine, and I realized the silence had grown uncomfortably long. I cleared my throat. "I only met your stepfather once. He was, er, an interesting guy."

"That's one way to put it. Do you have a vacant room?"

"You really don't want to go home?"

He gave an exaggerated shudder. "Oh, absolutely not. I love my mom, I do. But I can't listen to her fight with Nana. Especially over whether they should have given me a loan for business school. My stepfather refused, and Mom took his side."

"She did? That's terrible! You'd think Darren would be happy you wanted to go into business, be more like him."

"He probably would have been if my intended business was anything he respected. I wanted to open my own bar."

"Oh, really? We don't have a good bar around here." There were two nearby, but one catered to a rougher crowd, and the other was full of college kids. I never felt as ancient as after an evening spent drinking there.

Or a half-hour, as it turned out.

"I know. This was a while ago. I wanted to buy the place in Shady Grove, turn it into something special. But it never happened."

"It's not too late. Last I heard, the building was empty."

His eyes lit up. "You're serious? It's been years."

"I know. My friend told me people have tried to get it running, but it always fails. Everyone thinks it's cursed. Now no one will touch it. Ridiculous, right? But that's good news for you. It's been empty so long, you could probably get it for a steal."

He struck a pose. "I ain't afraid of no ghosts."

That made me laugh, both because of the reference and because I could picture Walter pretending to take offense. If he were around, anyway. Where had he gone off to? He'd been irritated with Darren, but rarely stayed away this long.

A massive TV hung in the lobby, and streaming didn't exist during my grandfather's lifetime. That lure was usually enough to keep him coming back. If he was hiding, he must be upset.

Darren was less amused. "Does that line get women? What a joke."

I tried to subtly roll my eyes at Darren to let him know Ben wasn't hitting on me. Instead, I wound up making such a weird face at Ben that he looked down at the counter to avoid my eyes.

Turning to my computer, I tapped around a bit, knowing darn well most of the rooms were empty. The majority of people who inquired about a room got referred to Toby's place—he needed the money. But I preferred to keep Ben close.

The key I took from beneath the counter hung on a woven fob. I'd carded the wool myself, woven the thread, made the cloth, and sewn the whole thing with a layer of magic. It was spelled to warn me when the holder approached, a way of not being taken by surprise. Before passing the key to Ben, I whispered a quick charm to engage the magic.

"What was that?"

"Oh, um... old Irish proverb. Just a silly prayer wishing you safe travels." I handed him the fob. "Upstairs. Second room on the left. Bathroom is attached. Breakfast is served at eight in the morning. Josie usually puts out sandwiches or snacks for lunch, then dinner's at six, if you're around. All meals are included."

Darren squawked. "What? You're feeding him! Now he'll never leave. Come on, at least charge the kid for the food."

"Thanks, Emma."

"You're welcome. Let me know if you need anything."

"Right now, I need a quiet space. You've given me that, so thank you." He turned and headed up the stairs.

I watched him go, hoping I'd made the right decision.

EIGHTEEN

About an hour after Ben finished checking in, the entry bells jingled again. We were rarely busy, so this was unusual. When I turned toward the door, Tim stood there.

"Hey. Good to see you again," I said. "Unless you're here to arrest me or one of my friends."

His cheeks turned red. "Great news! You're off the hook."

"Gee, thanks. What convinced you?"

"We found the killer."

That made me choke on my coffee. It took almost a full minute to catch my breath. "Already? That's quick." So quick I wondered if they had an investigative witch on the force, using magic to track the culprit.

Tim nodded. "We caught a lucky break. A fingerprint on an employee exit matched Casey Springfield, who does not work there. When confronted, she confessed to everything."

Beside me, Darren stiffened. "My Casey?"

The name sounded familiar, but Tim shouldn't know I'd been doing my own digging. "Who is that?"

"Darren's former assistant, laid off a few months ago."

"I thought she didn't hold a grudge," I said to Darren.

Part of me was frustrated that they'd figured things out before Darren and I got to talk to her. Once I started working on a puzzle, I liked to finish. But at least the mystery was solved.

Tim's eyes bored holes into my face. "How do you know how Casey felt?"

Uh-oh.

"Um, at the spa. When I met Darren, he said I reminded him of his assistant."

"How?" Tim's dubious expression somehow made me want to continue with the lie.

"We're both white women?" My voice raised in a way that made the lie obvious. I shot a helpless look at Darren. He must've been enjoying himself, because he grinned back.

I tried to signal with my eyes that I needed to know more about his former assistant, but he said, "Oh! Tell him you both live on planet Earth. You're practically twins."

"You met Darren at the spa, and he said you remind him of his former assistant because you're both white women. That didn't seem strange?"

"No, it definitely does. Did. And, oh, we both look good in white. Like the bathrobes."

It was amazing how the lies kept going once they got started. It was a good thing no one could ask Darren about this alleged conversation.

Tim's eyes narrowed. "What else did he tell you about Casey?"

I swallowed, my eyes darting helplessly to Darren.

"I like watching you squirm," he said.

"Um…" I took a big gulp of coffee to buy time, certain Tim would slap the cuffs on me at any minute.

Darren snorted. "Okay, fine. You're about the same height, you smile with your entire face, and you're both bossy. Like when you told me to get off the phone. That's all I've got."

After shooting him a look that hopefully conveyed my feelings about this sentiment, I repeated all of that. Tim nodded. What a relief.

Really, I should leave well enough alone, but I couldn't resist asking for details. After more than twenty-four hours of investigating, I'd earned this reward.

"How did she do it?"

"Slipped poison into his teacup when he was in that dark room. Brilliant, really. She found something slow-acting and lethal. She stuck around to make sure he drank it, then slid out the back. By the time the poison took effect, she was halfway home. I went to question her, and she confessed almost immediately."

"I'm glad you caught her. Um, did you find her prints on the teacup?" *Please say no, please say no.* If they found my prints beside the killer's, that would not look good.

He shook his head, and I tried not to let my relief show. "We never found the cup. By the time we arrived, someone had run the dishwasher. We pulled every mug in the load for testing, but I don't expect any usable results. The tox screen on the deceased should be enough to support her statement. No one else could have known the details."

"I hope you get it back soon," I said. "How did she get in?"

"Through the front door." Tim shook his head. "Once we got a name, we checked the log books. No appointment under that name, but we found one under Natasha Romanov."

"From the Marvel movies?"

"Yeah. I guess it didn't ring a bell when she booked it. She prepaid with a gift card, so she didn't have to provide a credit card number. Her service would have been after Darren was found, but they encourage people to arrive early and enjoy the facilities."

"Where did she get the card?"

"Bought online, this time with a Visa gift card. We traced the IP address to the public library in Saratoga."

"Did she have a reason to be in Saratoga?"

"Everyone has reason to be in Saratoga," Darren said. "Better restaurants, better entertainment, and I'm guessing you don't get murdered in their spas."

The guy had a point. Tim echoed his sentiment, but nicer.

"Sounds like this wasn't her first offense, if her prints were in the system."

"Do I look like someone who consorts with criminals?" Darren asked.

Tim shook his head. "That's the funny thing. We got lucky. One print, which matched a woman we arrested for a drunk and disorderly a few weeks ago."

"All because she got fired," I said under my breath. Imagine if she'd been aware Mrs. Cartwright insisted Darren let her go. Would he be alive? Would Angie?

"You never can figure out what makes some people tick, can you? At least the streets of Willow Falls will again be safe. The case is almost closed. I just need you to review and sign your statement for the file. If you could come down to the station tonight or tomorrow, I'd appreciate it."

"No problem," I said. This information could've been

conveyed by text, but I was glad to see him. "Thanks for dropping by."

Tim said, "Oh, sorry. I'm actually here on another matter."

"Couldn't wait to see me again?" I asked teasingly.

His cheeks turned red, and he avoided my gaze while reaching into his pocket. "Officer Peterson was going to come talk to you, but I've got her typing up the Cartwright report so I could do it instead. This matter needed a certain finesse that she doesn't always use."

"What's going on?"

"I'm investigating the disappearance of a young man from the Capital District."

My brow furrowed. The Capital District was a large area, but mostly referred to Albany and the immediate surrounding areas. We lived almost an hour north. "Isn't that a little outside your jurisdiction?"

"He was spotted in this area. This is an extensive property. I thought he might be hiding in one of the outbuildings. Maybe you saw something without realizing it was important."

"Well, obviously I wouldn't know if someone were hiding from me, but I haven't seen anything suspicious." Pink should tell me if he spotted a trespasser.

"I was afraid you'd say that. The thing is, his parents gave a description of the boy's bicycle. It disappeared when he did."

Something twisted in my stomach. We had a teenage boy and a bicycle here. But surely—

Tim pulled a picture out of his pocket. "Here we go. Witnesses saw you riding this bicycle not long after he went missing. That's why I'm here. Seventeen years old, Black, very tall, name Terrence."

When Tim slid the picture in front of me, my blood ran cold. T's face smiled back at me.

My mind raced, trying to figure out where I'd gone wrong. How could T be missing?

"Please don't tell me I've spent two days running around with a kidnapper," Darren said. "That's low."

"Good-looking kid," I said mildly.

"Yeah. That's an older picture. Here's a more recent one." Another image slid onto the counter in front of me. This picture captured T kneeling in the garden. Beside him, our faces clearly visible, stood me and Josie.

"There must be a mistake," I said desperately, knowing I'd been caught. Pretending I didn't know him would only make things worse. "T is eighteen. He told me he's eighteen."

"You asked for ID, right? Got a credit card and a driver's license before renting him a room. You know, like a businesswoman would."

Jinkies.

There wasn't anything to do but admit the truth. About this one thing, at least. I cleared my throat and leaned in, lowering my voice. "Can you keep a secret?"

"Do I need to read you your rights, Ms. Faden?"

"I dearly hope not. No, listen. I don't take ID. I don't ask for a credit card, or any money at all. This house is a sanctuary. Hence the sign outside."

"Haven," Tim said, more to himself than me. "I wondered about that. Has a nice ring. But you can't take in minors without parental consent."

"I didn't think I was. T said he didn't have anywhere to go. He's good with plants, so I told him he could stay as long as he helped in the garden."

"You didn't check?"

"Why would I? He told me he's an adult. And who would I call? We're not demanding references for people seeking refuge." I took a deep breath. "Asking lots of questions wouldn't encourage people to ask for help."

"Neither would being arrested for harboring a runaway."

One step forward, two steps back. Every time I thought we were getting closer, something like this pushed us further apart. But I stood my ground. Hoping he didn't see how much his lack of faith in me hurt, I threw my shoulders back and glared. "This foyer is open to the public, *Detective Pratt,* but unless you have a warrant, I'm going to have to ask you to leave. We have a right to refuse service to anyone."

He reached out and touched my hand. "Listen, I'm sorry. But Terrence has two parents, and they're searching for him."

"Are you sure about that? T told me his parents kicked him out."

"Maybe they changed their minds. Or maybe he lied." After I glared at him for several seconds, he sighed and shook his head. "Can I at least talk to the kid, get his side? I could call and get a warrant, but I'd prefer not to."

"Only if he agrees. If not, I'll scream 'lawyer' to the heavens."

"Fair enough. Where is he?"

"I have no idea." I met his eye squarely, daring him to call me out. But I saw a weariness there that made me feel bad. Tim was only doing his job. If T ran away from home, there might be better ways to help him than getting arrested. "I'll text him. But if he doesn't want to talk to you, you'll have to leave."

"I will leave if you arrange to have him contact me. But if he doesn't show up, I'll have to come back to get him."

Pulling out my phone, I texted T that Detective Pratt had some questions for him.

Say the word, and I'll tell him to stick it where the sun doesn't shine. I'll hire you a lawyer.

T's first response wasn't fit for polite company. Then he followed it with:

You like that dude, right?

We're friendly. Not the point. I'm on your side.

Thanks. I'll talk to him tomorrow. Toby needs me.

Will you come with?

Of course. I'm free when you are.

Perhaps Toby's influence over T was stronger than I thought. Facing the music was very mature of him.

"T said he's happy to sit down with both of us," I said. "He's going to be a few hours, though. Can we come to the station tomorrow?"

"Do you promise he'll show?"

"Girl Scout's honor." It seemed like the statement should come with a salute, but somehow I flashed the "live long and prosper" sign from *Star Trek*.

"You're an interesting woman, Emma. I can't figure you

out." Tim smiled, and once again, I was taken in by his gorgeous brown eyes. "There's a spark, I feel it. But I don't know if I can trust you."

"That's fair. Before I moved here, I didn't trust anyone."

"I was planning to wait to ask you out until you weren't at the center of one of my murder investigations. Or kidnapping. Any major felony, really."

My pulse raced, but I forced myself to sound casual. "Yeah? Any idea when that might be?"

"Sadly, no. I may have to ask the department to hire a second detective if I want a date this year."

"Well, if it's any consolation, I plan to never get accused of murder again. This should be the last time."

He ducked his head. "We have to cover ourselves. I didn't want anyone to think you were getting special treatment."

"That would be awful. They might suspect you like me." When he didn't answer, I leaned in and lowered my voice. "If it helps, I like you, too. You know, when you're ready."

"That helps. I'll keep it in mind." He cleared his throat. "I'm not very good at this. My wife left ten years ago, and I've been focused on my daughter ever since."

"Well, the last guy who caught my interest was a murderer, so I'm not winning any dating prizes."

"That's oddly comforting, you know? I may have my flaws—and plenty of them, as my ex-wife could tell you— but I absolutely, positively satisfy your not-a-murderer prerequisite."

I smiled at him. "At the moment, that's my single requirement. I'm all about pressure-free dating."

"Great." He started to walk away, then paused. "I'll be in touch."

"I can't wait."

After Tim left, I turned to Darren. "I suppose this is goodbye."

"What are you talking about?"

"They caught your killer. She gave a full confession. We resolved your earthly conflicts! I thought you'd want to move on now."

Darren looked up with so much intensity that my gaze followed, but there was nothing there other than the ceiling. "Shouldn't there be a light?"

"I think it's a door," I said, remembering when my late chef transitioned to the next plane.

"Maybe it's not time for me to go yet. This makes no sense. Why would Casey kill me? Yeah, I fired her, but we had a good relationship. I gave her a huge payout. Why risk everything to kill me months later?"

"When was the last time you talked to her?"

"The day she left." He shrugged. "Haven't thought about her since the severance payment left the bank."

"Maybe we can find out more." I went to my computer and typed "Casey Springfield" into the search bar, along with "drunk." Maybe the local newspaper in this sleepy town covered minor misdemeanors.

The first article that popped up named her as Darren's killer. News traveled at light speed in small towns—she'd barely been arrested before this reporter posted the story.

The piece contained only a little information, most of which we'd already learned from Tim. Casey's fingerprints were discovered at the scene; she had a history with the victim. Interestingly enough, the article made it sound like she spotted Darren at the spa and seized the opportunity for revenge. Nothing about using a fake name.

"Bull." Darren jabbed a finger at the image on the screen. "She happened to be at the spa? No way. She knew Tuesdays were my morning with Eve. Casey used to make the appointments."

"She took an enormous risk. What if you'd spotted her?" I studied him for a minute. "You didn't see her, right?"

"Nah. Dark room, big place. And I was on the phone."

"You're saying if you'd followed the spa rules and turned your device off, you might have spotted the woman who poisoned you before it happened? If that's not a good reason—"

"Shut your trap, would you? Even if I'd seen her, I wouldn't have expected her to kill me."

"Why does it matter? The evidence fits. She confessed, and she knew exactly how it happened. Do you care why?"

"It makes no sense. You don't understand. Casey and I got along. Not like Angie feared, but we worked well together."

"Fine." I went to the New York court system's website and searched for her name. A docket sheet popped up. Drunk and disorderly was a minor offense. No prior record.

According to the court records, she pleaded guilty and took community service instead of a fine.

"This isn't helping," Darren snapped. "Let me do it."

"Sure, no problem." I pushed away from the computer and leaned back, folding my arms. "Knock yourself out."

Pink jumped up on the desk and stretched out across the top. "Is it wise to antagonize the ghost?"

"Trust me, I'm not the antagonist here," I said with a glance at my uninvited guest. "Where's Walter?"

"What's wrong? Can't take a little criticism?" Darren asked.

"He doesn't want to be around someone who intentionally alienates him," I replied. "Can't you try to get along with people?"

"Why should I? He's mad that I sat on him when I didn't even know he was there."

"You got mad when Dottie teleported onto—"

Pink meowed. "Children! Must I separate you?"

"I wish you could," I muttered.

"Walter is fine," Pink said to me. "Showing himself to anyone, even you, requires energy. Bouncing back to the mansion yesterday used more. He's trying to hide it, but he's tired. It'll do him some good to rest. When he feels better, he'll be back."

"Hey, that reminds me," I said. "Why is Walter is tied to the house, but Darren can follow me around?"

"Listen, I don't want to be here, either," Darren said. "I wanted to go to the office."

"I need to understand how this works."

Pink studied Darren for a moment before he spoke. "Darren is here temporarily. Once you find his killer, he should move on. He's not tied to any specific location."

"And Walter? Doesn't he have unfinished business?"

"Your grandfather is a special case. He wanted to meet you. He used his powers to remain here as a ghost."

"What happens to people who never finish their business? Are there ghosts everywhere?"

"The vast majority of people move on without help. Sometimes when a ghost suffers a traumatic death, like murder, they get stuck here. They usually remain in a place related to the trauma. That's why we hear tales of haunted houses. You should talk to Walter about this. After all, he's the source of your power."

"Excuse me," Darren shouted. "This mumbo jumbo is fascinating and all, but—"

Pink gave him a scathing look. "You are a ghost conversing with a cat in a witch's home, and you dare to use the phrase 'mumbo jumbo' to refer to us?"

"How do I know you're real? Maybe I'm hallucinating. This could be a dream. I bet I'm still on the massage table."

"I dearly wish that were the case," I said. "How would you hallucinate me and my powers?"

"That's exactly what a hallucination would say."

Pink snorted.

I gave him a pleading look. "See why I'm ready for Darren to move on?"

"So solve the case. Set him free," Pink said.

"The case is solved. Detective Pratt said so not five minutes ago."

Darren gestured at himself. "Then what am I still doing here? I'm telling you, something smells fishy. Casey wasn't mad at me. She was fine. If we'd interviewed her yesterday, you never would've considered her a suspect. Why would she kill me?"

"I don't know. Why don't you go ask her?" I said darkly.

"Emma…" Pink dragged my name out the way Grandma Vera used to when I was about to get in trouble.

"That's a great idea! Come on!" Darren said.

"I was being sarcastic. You can't."

"Maybe not, but you can," he said. "She got locked up, right? Let's go to the station."

I shook my head, turning back to the computer. There had to be something we missed, but one search after another turned up no helpful results. I tried "Casey + the advertising agency," "Casey + Darren," and "Casey + William," then did all the same searches with last names. Nothing explained why this woman would kill Darren months after getting fired. Even if the severance ran out, murder didn't fix that.

"The best way to learn her motive," Pink said, watching my frustration grow. "Is to ask her."

"Don't help," I said to my cat.

In response, he lifted one leg and licked the inside. "You're the one who wanted our guest to move on. Either the police are missing something about the murder, or Darren has other unfinished business. Either way, talk to Casey."

With a sigh, I grabbed my car keys off the desk and hopped to my feet. "Let's go. Darren, you have five minutes to figure out how to explain why I want to see her."

TWENTY

In a small town like Willow Falls, we reached the local police station in minutes. Darren and I arrived so quickly, we hadn't come up with a reason for me to speak to Casey.

When Josie had been falsely arrested, Tim let me see her because we were friends and because the murder occurred in my house. Now, although I'd found the body, I didn't have any solid connection to the victim, the crime scene, or the killer.

"Do you need a reason to visit someone in a holding cell?" Darren asked as I turned onto Main Street. "What if you want to interview her for the local paper?"

"Then I should call an actual journalist and send them in. Tim knows I'm not a reporter." After finding a space on the street near the rear of the building, I shifted into park and tapped the steering wheel thoughtfully. "Why don't you go in?"

"Because, as you so thoughtfully pointed out earlier, she won't see or hear me. Thanks for the reminder."

"I don't mean for a conversation," I said. "You don't

need permission to wander around. You can listen with no one knowing. She might be getting interrogated by the police or talking to her lawyer. Go in, look around, listen. You might overhear something useful."

"That's the dumbest plan I've ever heard."

Honking horns drew my attention away from the scathing retort that surely would have come to me. In the intersection ahead, a light blue minivan swerved, narrowly avoiding getting T-boned by oncoming traffic. From what I could see, the driver ran the red light.

The vehicle swung wildly into the parking lot, almost sideswiping a parked police cruiser. A blonde woman about my age me sat behind the wheel. She pulled into one of the visitor spaces, somehow being over the line on both sides. I wondered if she was turning herself in for drunk driving.

"Hold on a sec," Darren said. "I know her."

"Are you sure?" Bumper stickers on the back of the van proudly informed me that the owner's children were honor students at Willow Falls Elementary.

"Yeah. She used to bring Casey lunch sometimes. They were friends."

"Okay, then." When the woman walked toward the rear entrance on shaking legs, I knew he must be right. "There's our chance."

"You want me to scare her?" Darren asked.

"Don't be ridiculous. She must be here for Casey. Listen to their conversation. If she explains to her friend why she killed you, maybe you'll get closure."

"Where do I go?" Now that we had a plan, he seemed unsure.

I pointed at a section of the brick wall with small rectangular windows near the top. "Those are the holding cells. Go through here first. I'll be on the other side."

"What if I need you?"

"Come back out. Or yell, see if I hear you through the walls. But you're not in any danger, and no one will spot you. I can't say the same."

He sighed. "If this is how you manage a team, it's good you inherited your money."

Through gritted teeth, I said, "We're not a team. Go."

Finally, Darren passed through the brick wall into the back of the building. If Casey wasn't being questioned, she'd be there. When I'd visited Josie at the station a few weeks ago, the officers hadn't brought her into a separate room. We'd talked through the bars.

Since I couldn't hear anything while inside my car, I got out and casually strolled toward the area where Darren had vanished. Leaning against the wall, I did my best to appear inconspicuous.

With nothing else to do, I pulled out my phone. Instead of looking for more information on Casey, I typed T's full name into my search bar. According to Tim, he'd run away from home. According to my friend, his parents threw him out. Either way, he needed help.

The first result was from the Albany Times-Union. "Local Teen Reported Missing." My heart stuttered. According to the article, T was a senior in high school. His family lived in Troy, which was a local suburb and also the town where Uncle Sam was born. Teachers described him as a bright kid, polite and easygoing. That all tracked with the person staying at Haven. But where T told me he was a high school graduate, this article said he'd started missing classes at the beginning of the semester. Arriving late, leaving at lunchtime, things like that. After about a month, he'd stopped showing up at all. The article confirmed everything Tim told me.

In September, a mysterious bike showed up in my barn. Then T appeared, saying a mutual friend told him I could help. We'd agreed he could stay in exchange for taking care of the garden.

A pit formed in my stomach when I realized everything he'd told me was a lie. I'd trusted him because he'd arrived with a referral from someone I trusted. Now the police might charge me with kidnapping a minor.

Not knowing what else to do, I called Olive Green, who lived in Shady Grove and owned the antique store where my friend worked. She volunteered at the LGBT Teen Center and, according to T, she'd directed him my way. Maybe I should have done this sooner, but I'd wanted to trust him.

She answered immediately. "Emma! It's always a pleasure. How are you, dear?"

"Um, I'm okay. Listen, do you know a kid named T?"

"Of course! He found you, did he?"

"Yeah, he did. He's been staying at Haven for a few weeks now. Last night, the police showed up, claiming he's a runaway. I don't know what to do. Do I send him home?"

"If the police find him, you won't have a choice," she said.

A heavy sigh escaped me. "I know. And Tim saw us together. T wasn't there, but at some point, I have to bring him to the police station or get in more trouble. What do I do?"

"I suggest you have a talk with T."

"Aly mentioned once that you're great at making her figure out her own problems," I grumbled. "Living up to the legacy."

She laughed. "I have faith in you."

At least that made one of us. Not feeling any better, I

debated texting T before deciding to talk to him in person once Darren moved on to the afterlife. One enormous problem at a time.

A few minutes later, Darren popped out of the wall. "You will not *believe* what just happened!"

"Did Casey lie about killing you?" I couldn't imagine why she would give a false confession, but it would explain his excitement level.

"No, better!" Before I could ask what he meant, he continued, "That patsy was paid to take the fall!"

My eyes widened. "What? Are you sure? Why would she do that?"

"I heard the whole thing. Casey's got a brain tumor. Inoperable. She found out a few weeks ago. That's why she killed me."

My brain wasn't following. "You gave her a brain tumor?"

"No! Someone paid her to do it. Her mom is in a nursing home. Late stage dementia. Casey was worried there wouldn't be anyone to pay for her mom's care. Now, she's set."

"Who would pay someone to kill you?" Perhaps the better question was, who had that much money and how did they know Casey?

"She wouldn't say. The friend said she was gonna go straight to Pratt and tell him, get Casey released. She's mad. Casey begged her to keep quiet. Said her mom would lose the money if anyone found out."

My heart broke more at every word. The dates lined up. The drunk and disorderly arrest must have happened right after Casey got the news. If I got that diagnosis, I'd get really drunk, too. Casey didn't have a secret reason for hating Darren. She'd been a victim of circumstance. No wonder he felt unsettled—the mastermind behind his death was still unknown.

Footsteps on the pavement made me realize I'd stopped pretending to read on my phone. Someone cleared their throat behind me. The blood drained from my face. I turned around and spotted Officer Peterson on the sidewalk, not three feet away.

She rested one hand on the gun strapped to her hip as she asked, "What are you doing here? Who are you talking to?"

Thinking fast, I grasped for any plausible reason for me to be standing in the middle of the sidewalk, having a conversation with no one. "Hello, Officer. How are you?"

"Fine, Ms. Faden. Why are you standing outside the police station talking to yourself? Did you come to confess?"

TWENTY-ONE

Everyone thought magical powers were so cool, but no one realized how taxing it could be to keep such an enormous secret. Especially when I kept finding myself around people trained to be observant. Not only had Officer Peterson seen me at the heart of two murders since moving to town three months ago, but she hated me. If I wasn't careful, she'd have me locked up as a danger to myself and others.

Rather than answer her question, I deflected, "What are you talking about?"

"You're in trouble now," Darren said.

She gestured toward the street. "You parked in front of the station fifteen minutes ago. You sat in the car so long you might have been casing the joint. Instead of coming in, you walked around the back. Ever since, you've been walking around, gesturing, and talking. But there's no one else here."

"I'm flattered by your interest in me, Officer. I didn't know you cared."

"Don't be cute. I meant what I said earlier: I'm going to find out how you're involved in this."

"Didn't someone else confess?"

"I don't know if she acted alone. Maybe there was a bigger conspiracy."

Rather than explain my eavesdropping ghost, I reached for a plausible excuse. "Other than finding the body, I'm not involved. That's why I'm here. I told Detective Pratt I'd review my formal statement for the file."

She smirked. "For the file, eh? Then you won't mind giving it to me."

"I thought you'd have more important things to do than play secretary for the detectives."

She flinched. Then she turned toward the station and held out one arm. "After you."

Inside, Officer Gutierrez sat at the front desk, gazing intently at a Sudoku book. When Officer Peterson stopped to ask him if we could have an available conference room, he smiled up at her, as if relieved at the interruption.

"Can I come?" he asked hopefully. "It's dead out here."

She laughed, a sound that seemed foreign coming from her. "That's what you get for eating the chief's turkey sub. Enjoy riding the desk."

"It's not like I knew it was hers," he grumbled before turning back to the book. "Room one is open."

We'd made it halfway across the room when someone called her name, bringing us both to a halt. Tim walked toward us. To my surprise, Officer Peterson looked disappointed to see him. I realized why when Tim said her assistance wasn't needed.

"I'll take things from here," Tim said. "Thank you for bringing Emma inside."

"It's no problem—"

"You can go, Officer. I've developed a rapport with this witness, and she *is* here to meet me."

Gritting her teeth, Officer Peterson said goodbye to Tim and turned to go. When she walked by me, her eyes shot daggers. Her shoulder checked me on the way past. It couldn't have been accidental.

"I don't think she likes me," I said mildly. No reason to explain that she thought I flirted with him too much. "Thanks for saving me."

"Saving? I have no idea what you're talking about. I like to take my own statements in case I have follow-up questions." He winked at me.

I followed him into the conference room. Although on TV these rooms contained a giant one-way mirror, the door opened into a three-by-four-foot rectangle with a small table in the middle, chairs on either side, and a teeny window in the door. Video cameras in both corners made it easy for other officers to observe from anywhere.

Tim gestured to the chair furthest from the door, then sat across from me. If I wanted to leave, I'd have to walk by him. Then he pulled out a recorder. "If you don't mind, I'll capture everything you say. Later, we'll transcribe it and give it to you for approval and signature."

"Don't you have the statement I gave earlier?"

"I have my notes, but I'd like to get it on tape."

"No problem." I took a deep breath. "In the middle of my massage—"

"No, no. Start at the beginning."

"Sure, I met the deceased a few minutes before Eve took him to his service. He sat in the chair beside mine."

"And you spoke?"

Remembering my earlier deception, I said, "Yeah. We did."

"What did he tell you about Ms. Springfield? This is important, for the record."

The blood drained out of my face. "For my official statement? The one sworn to under oath."

"Right. It'll form the basis for your testimony at trial. You know, given under penalty of perjury."

Closing my eyes, I shook my head. The lies had gone too far. I couldn't put an entire fake interaction in writing and testify to it in court.

"Just do it," Darren said. "Who will a little white lie hurt?"

"What's wrong, Emma?"

I opened my eyes and looked at Tim. He knew. I'd have bet all of Walter's money that he knew I lied about my conversation with Darren before he died.

"Nothing. I'd just prefer to start with finding the body. Establish the timeline."

"We talked to all the witnesses and everyone said your interaction with Darren in the Relaxation Room was brief and not cordial." He dropped his voice to a whisper, still gazing intently at me. "Never lie to me again. This statement better be true, or I'll lock you up faster than you can blink. Do you understand?"

With a gulp, I nodded. So much for our friendship blossoming.

This time, when I started going over my interaction with Darren in the Relaxation Room before my appointment, Tim let me speak. I stuck to the facts, only omitting Walter's actions and statements. He interrupted a few times with questions. At the end, he recapped for the recording, then asked a few clarifying questions. Finally, he let me know we had enough to put everything in writing.

Outside the conference room, Tim gave the recorder to Officer Gutierrez along with his notes and asked him to type up the statement. Poor Officer Gutierrez seemed relieved to have work. Then Tim asked me to wait in his office until the statement was ready.

"I can stay in the conference room."

"No, if we're going to chat, my office is more comfortable. Come on." He led me into a smallish room dominated by a corner desk with multiple monitors on it. Carefully stacked papers sat in several piles on one side of the desk. Everything lined up perpendicularly. Picture frames pointed away from the entrance, so I couldn't see them— probably his daughter.

After I sat in the uncomfortable wooden chair provided for visitors, Tim closed the door and shut the blinds covering his window. My mind flashed wildly toward the idea that he was going to set me on the desk and ravish me, but this wasn't a romance novel. Instead, he sat at his desk, looking very uncomfortable until he loosened his tie.

While I waited for him to explain why he'd asked me to wait here, I asked the silken threads of his tie to loosen. They resisted at first, but I was learning firm persistence.

Darren walked through the desk, swiping at papers as if to knock them over. Unfortunately for him, nothing moved. Not even a breeze marked his passage. Then he went to the monitors and crouched to read them. I didn't realize how long I'd been watching the ghost until I noticed Tim staring.

Awkwardly, I cleared my throat. "How can I help you?"

"We need to talk. I don't think you killed anyone, but I know you're hiding something."

"What do you mean?"

"When I was at your place earlier, Officer Gutierrez reviewed the video from the spa. He saw everything."

"That's great! You mean you caught Casey on camera?"

"Not exactly. We saw Eve take Darren into the room. She left, maybe fifteen to twenty minutes later."

"That's what she was going to get the massage oil?"

"Right. That's not the weird part. No one else entered the room until you arrived. Then Eve came back, followed by Suzanne Bracken. According to the timestamp, you all left a couple of minutes before she called 911."

"Everything sounds normal," I said. "No one else came in?"

"Nope. Not even someone walking by. No movement at all." He shook his head. "That would have been helpful. There's no other entrance. We checked."

"Could someone go through the ceiling tiles?" It happened in the movies.

"Hypothetically? Sure, maybe. Nothing points to that, though, and there wasn't much time."

"Casey said she poisoned Darren's cup in the Relaxation Room, didn't she? Based on what you're saying, that seems like the most likely explanation."

"Funny you should say that. I saw something very unlikely on those tapes."

That made me sit up straighter. "What?"

"The camera outside Missy's room shows you going in together. She leaves and comes back holding a paper cup. Twenty minutes go by; she leaves again. All of a sudden, the door flies open. You race out the door like your hair is on fire."

My cheeks flamed. I couldn't meet his gaze. Oh, I should go. The thought that the guy I might like saw me running down a public hallway naked made me wish the floor would open up and swallow me. "You saw me. Without clothes."

"The video was grainy. You couldn't see much. That's not the point. I know this sounds crazy, but hear me out. Your robe followed you down the hall."

TWENTY-TWO

A weak laugh escaped me. "That's hilarious. Obviously a trick of the light. How would my robe move on its own?"

"An excellent question. I'd also like to know how you got up while fully swaddled, and why you sprinted down the hall."

"I jerked the towels up. You can still move your arms while wrapped. I didn't know how much force to use."

"Right. Because you desperately needed to use the bathroom." His tone suggested he'd be more likely to believe me if I claimed to be Dr. Strange.

"When you've got to go, you've got to go, right?"

"I don't think that's it." Tim shook his head. "Listen, you need to be straight with me. I need to be able to trust you."

"I'm not a killer."

"It's more than that. When you were on the sidewalk outside, who were you talking to?"

"I was on the phone with Josie."

"Sure you were. I guess you have Bluetooth earbuds."

He held a hand out before I could agree. "Do you mind showing me your call history?"

"Don't do it! Tell him you're a sovereign citizen!" Darren shouted.

With great effort, I pressed my lips together, hoping Tim thought I looked annoyed rather than highly amused. "Yes, I mind. You don't have a warrant. Besides, even if I was talking to myself, that's not a crime."

"You're right, it's not." He turned in Darren's direction. "Why are you always speaking to empty air?"

"Huh?"

"When I was at the bed-and-breakfast earlier, you kept looking over my shoulder like someone was standing there. Only there wasn't. You were sitting on the chaise at the spa alone, but your lips were moving. Now, Officer Peterson saw you talking to no one. I went to the window, and lo-and-behold—she was right."

"It's a coping mechanism," I said. "Saying things out loud calms me."

His smile dropped, and he let silence descend. The moving second hand on the clock was deafening while I waited for him to speak. Tick, tick, tick. Betrayal shone in Tim's eyes. His expression made my stomach twist into knots. With each second that ticked by, our blossoming "relationship" withered. Losing the potential for something more made me sad.

Finally, Tim said, "Okay, fine. Too bad. I thought you might be talking to Darren's ghost."

My jaw dropped. I closed it with effort, but it took a long time before I managed the fakest-sounding laugh anyone ever uttered. "Ghosts! Don't be ridiculous. Ghosts aren't real. Why would there be a ghost? How? And what makes you think I can see him?"

"A lot of strange things happen around here, Emma," Tim said. "My daughter's friend is psychic. You were definitely lying earlier. A ghost seemed like the most logical conclusion."

I couldn't speak. Aly kept her abilities a secret. I never considered that the police detective in the next town would know her personally or know about her powers. His daughter was the right age, though. He must be talking about Aly.

When Tim realized I was incapable of opening my mouth and forming words, he continued, "I have no problem with ghosts. Ghosts are cool. Lies are not. Incidentally, you should know you're a terrible liar. Your eyes give you away. I'd have known you were lying even if we hadn't checked your story."

At this, I felt a weird mixture of shame and relief. At least I could drop the facade. "Am I under arrest?"

"No. You're free to go. But I hope you'll stay."

"Run. Leave now," Darren said.

Tim asked, "How do you take your coffee?"

If I left now, we'd never be anything other than acquaintances. I didn't want to give up that easily. "Is it powdered creamer?"

"I think so, yeah."

I grimaced. The powdered stuff tasted like armpits. "Black is fine."

Once we both had our beverages, he re-settled behind his desk and met my eyes squarely. "I did some digging."

The intensity of his stare made me want to avert my eyes, but I forced myself to hold steady. "On me?"

"Of course on you. First, Tiffaneigh tells me you won the Annual Shady Grove Treasure Hunt, which everyone thought was rigged. The clues were literally impossible to solve. Some were written in a made-up language. The likelihood of a stranger showing up and solving them was zero."

"Oh, that's nothing," I said. "I'm very good at riddles. None of my friends would play Clue with me as a kid because I always won."

He continued as if I hadn't spoken. "Then you move here, and someone dies. You know things about the victim you couldn't have known. Now you've found a second body, and you're constantly talking to someone who isn't there. When we arrested Cliff last month, he swore up and down he'd been attacked by something invisible, and then your cat jinxed him. I don't know how much of that is true, but you're hiding something."

Either Tim was an excellent detective, or I wasn't as sly as I thought. Probably both.

"If you tell him, he might have you locked up in a psych ward," Darren said.

"He already knows," I said, glad not to have to hide it anymore. I had one friend in this town. If I never admitted the truth to anyone, that number couldn't grow.

Tim glanced at the space beside him, blinked a few times, then shook his head.

I let out a breath. "You're right. I can see ghosts. Walter Crow lives in the mansion with me, and last month, I saw Martha after her death. Darren's been following me around since I found him. I heard him screaming. That's why I jumped up. It seemed weird that no one else went to help until he turned out to be dead."

Tim nodded. "I'd been trying to figure out how you wandered into a crime scene in the middle of a spa service. Especially a service where you wrapped up tight. Even if you were looking for a bathroom, you walked past one to wind up in Eve's room."

"Please don't tell anyone. It's hard enough to fit in as the new girl in town. Incidentally, it wasn't a ghost that attacked Cliff. But, um, if you spend much around me, you'll probably see more stuff that can't be easily explained."

"I look forward to it," he said. "Your secret's safe with me."

"You seem to be taking this awfully well," I said.

"Like I said—Tiff's got a psychic friend. Weird things happen around here. Also, I saw the robe flying."

My cheeks grew warm. "I don't have a logical explanation for that. Sorry."

"I forgive you. Did Darren tell you how he died?"

I shook my head. "He doesn't remember. We were trying to identify who his enemies were, anyone with a motive. We actually talked about Casey, but Darren said she didn't harbor a grudge. She got a big severance package, seemed fine with it. I wanted to interview her anyway, but you arrested her before we got a chance."

"Tell him about the money!" Darren yelled. "Someone paid her!"

"If we hadn't found the fingerprint, it might have been a long time before she popped up on our radar," Tim said. "We might never have known who booked the fake appointment."

"Seems like a lucky break."

"Maybe. Tell me something. Before I told you about Casey, who did you think killed Darren?"

"Why? You've got her."

"Humor me. Please."

"Okay, but if you're hiring a new detective, you should

know that my plate is pretty full." He chuckled. After taking a fortifying sip of my coffee, I began. "Eve. Angie, before we found out about the fundraiser. Or possibly William. Suzanne, the spa owner."

"Not the son-in-law?"

"Nah. As much as Ben and Darren didn't like each other, my gut says he wasn't involved. Besides, he was also at the fundraiser."

"You're just swayed by his pretty face," Darren grumbled. "He's too young for you, you know. I bet you a thousand dollars that twerp killed me."

"Darren disagrees, for what it's worth. Ben hates him."

"True," Tim said. "He freely admits it. Why the masseuse?"

I summarized the evidence against each suspect, then pointed out that my most likely suspects weren't at the spa. "Angie and Ben were at a charity luncheon. It's all over Facebook. She was hosting, he tended bar, and they were both there all morning."

"Yeah, we confirmed their alibis early. You know, because that's what police officers do."

My cheeks grew red. "I was only trying to help."

"Thanks, Detective," he said with a wink. "Who else did you investigate for me?"

"William is on a business trip. I even asked Darren if he could have snuck back into town, but it didn't seem likely. Someone would have noticed if he had missed an entire day at the conference. We looked at Missy, too, since she disliked Darren so much. Not much evidence there."

"I can check into that, but you've got good instincts," Tim said, leaning back in his chair. "You've identified the people who seem most likely to me, too."

"You mean, other than Casey?"

"Not most likely to have poisoned Darren. Most likely to have paid her to do it."

That he'd come to this conclusion without a ghostly eavesdropper impressed me. "How did you know?"

"You don't seem surprised. We'll circle back on that," he said. "Catching Casey was too easy. She confessed immediately. Something felt off about it. Then we found out her mom lives in a nursing facility. Huge bills, very past due account, which mysteriously got paid in full a few days ago."

"That's what Casey told her friend." I explained Darren's eavesdropping.

"Everything fits," Tim said. "Eve wouldn't have access to the blunt. Same with Ben. But the wife and the brother-in-law do. Now you tell me they've got motives, too. An ironclad alibi seems like a great way to avoid suspicion."

"Have you checked the bank records?"

"Don't do it," Darren said.

"Do what?" I asked.

"You're going to tell him about my second set of books."

"It might be relevant, you know. Maybe William hired Casey, then left town. What if you were killed for cooking the books?"

Tim raised his eyebrows. "He was embezzling?"

"There's a false set of records in his desk at the office. I left it there, although *someone* was determined to get me to destroy it."

"Good thing you didn't."

"I am inherently a rule follower," I said. "I bend rules a bit to help people in need, but I wasn't about to make myself look guiltier."

Tim picked up his phone and pushed a few buttons.

After a moment, he said, "Gutierrez. Get a warrant for the ad agency's offices. Check the victim's desk drawers."

"In the very bottom drawer," I said helpfully.

"Traitor," Darren muttered.

"Can Mr. Cartwright think of anything else?" Tim asked.

"My useless stepson!" Darren shouted.

"Not liking Ben isn't helpful," I said.

"No, listen. I figured it out."

"You figured out how the unemployed bartender scraped together enough money to pay for a murder? Because I, for one, would love to know."

Tim cocked his head. "The stepson? Interesting."

"Darren's saying that because he doesn't like Ben."

"I am not," Darren said, as if Tim could hear him. "Listen. Years ago, Angie opened up a joint account with her son. Around the time he dropped out of school. She's been making deposits ever since. A hundred here, five hundred there. Tens of thousands of dollars. Does that kid look like he's got loads of money to you?"

"Maybe he's saving up for something special," I said, but repeated Darren's theory to Tim.

"Special like murder?" He rubbed his chin. "I'll get a subpoena for the bank records. His and his mom's. Too bad we can't have a ghost sign a consent form."

"Use my login," Darren said. "The bank probably hasn't disabled it yet."

I relayed his offer to Tim, but he stopped me halfway. "A police officer can't search bank records without a warrant. The evidence would get kicked out, and we might lose the whole case. I also can't authorize you to log into someone else's accounts, and you can't prove to a judge that the deceased's *ghost* gave you permission."

"Have I mentioned that I hate when you make sense?"

"I run my investigations by the book. I'll submit a request and wait to see what comes back, but it might be nothing. Casey will be arraigned tomorrow. Chief Yu wants to get ahead of the story. She called a press conference to announce we caught the killer. I told her I think there's more to it, but she insisted the investigation is closed."

"You're saying that, even if you get the records, you won't look at them?"

"I'll do my best, but it'll have to be solid to get the chief to look into a coconspirator. The sooner, the better."

"Then I better go see what I can find out before tomorrow morning."

Tim moved around his desk to hold the door open. "You will not. Go home, lock your doors, run your bed-and-breakfast, and stay safe. I don't want another call that someone tried to kill you."

"Neither do I," I breathed. "Neither do I."

"He's got a thing for you," Darren said when the door closed behind us.

"Hush," I said, trying not to move my mouth. "He thinks I'm a weirdo who talks to ghosts. We haven't even gotten to my magical abilities yet. He'd be a fool not to run."

"Then maybe he's a fool."

TWENTY-THREE

When Darren and I entered the mansion, Ben was watching TV in the lobby. "You don't mind, do you? My mom called. They're about to make an announcement about her husband's killer."

Interesting that he referred to Darren as his mother's husband rather than his stepfather. Was he trying to distance himself?

On the screen, an empty podium stood in front of the police station. To the right, a woman in her fifties spoke with someone off screen. She wore a perfectly pressed police uniform, much crisper than the one sported by Officer Gutierrez. Maybe Chief Yu kept a spare in her office. Or she might have gone home to change. The Willow Falls Chief of Police didn't give a press conference about murder every day.

It hadn't even occurred to me to talk to Ben after Tim gave me the news about Casey. It was his stepfather who died, after all. I glanced at him guiltily, but he was looking back and forth between the TV screen and his phone.

I moved to the couch and sank down near him. "Is your mom at the station?"

"Yeah, I think so. I told her to stay home, that the media will harass her, but she wants to put on a brave face. Let the people at the foundation see how strong she is." He shook his head. "Appearance is everything."

"As long as she doesn't confront the killer, it should be okay, right?"

"A media frenzy can be pretty bad. She's fragile right now."

The feed switched to another angle, clearly revealing Angie speaking with Chief Yu. Another woman stood beside them, her back to the camera. Twin gray braids wrapped around her head suggested she was older than them. She wore a long, flowing caftan covered in stars and moons. The TV wasn't picking up their conversation, but as she spoke, her arms waved emphatically to punctuate each word. Rings on each finger glittered in the light.

"Is that your grandmother?" I asked, remembering that she'd been visiting.

Ben snorted. "Nana wouldn't be caught dead at the police station. That's Pansy."

"Pansy?"

"Mom's psychic."

"Wait." I tried to keep my eyes trained on Ben, but my words were for his stepfather. "Angie really believes in psychics? Ghosts, spirits, mediums, all that jazz?"

"Told you," Darren said.

Ben shot me a look. "She's my mother. I may think Pansy is a con artist, but don't mock her beliefs. We don't know what's out there."

"Oh, no, it's not that. I'm just…" There was no way to end this sentence appropriately.

For a second, I longed for my memory-wiping cloth. I needed to talk to Darren, away from Ben's ears.

Standing up, I offered Ben a drink from the kitchen. He declined, but I went in, anyway. Darren followed. Luckily, Ben stayed put, eyes riveted to the television. The second the door closed behind me, I turned on the ghost. "I thought Angie passed out because she was so shocked to hear that ghosts were real, and you'd come to visit. If your wife believes in all this stuff, why did she faint? She should have been delighted to meet someone who could communicate with you."

"Like I said before, she never expected confirmation? How would you feel if aliens landed?"

"Excited? Confused? That's not the point." I waved a hand toward the living room. "When I said I was talking to your ghost, she should have been excited. Asking questions, looking for messages from the man she loves. Instead, she fainted."

He shrugged. "She doesn't eat much at those fundraisers, gets so busy. It could have been the stress of my death, plus no food."

While those could cause fainting, the timing was too convenient. Something seemed wrong. "What if she believed me?"

"What do you mean?"

Walter appeared at my elbow. "She means maybe your wife didn't faint because she found out ghosts were real. Maybe she was afraid of what *your* ghost planned to say."

I pictured the foyer. "When she fell, she seemed absolutely normal, just with her eyes closed. Breath steady, pulse a little faster than I expected."

"Did that seem fishy to you?"

"No. I'm not a doctor. My experience with people fainting is pretty much that one incident."

"Generally, fainting happens when a person's blood pressure drops. She would have had a slow heart rate, maybe even stopped breathing. Her vital signs shouldn't have remained normal."

Before I could ask him where he picked up this medical knowledge, Darren interrupted. "Thank you, Dr. Ghost. Why would she pretend to pass out?"

"To distract Emma," Walter said. "Give her time to think and deflect. Especially if you told Emma who killed you."

"I don't know who killed me!" Darren protested.

"She wouldn't know that," I said. "Why would you accuse her, though? Even if Darren had seen Casey at the spa, he couldn't have implicated his wife."

"Maybe Casey was supposed to say, 'This is for Angie!' as she slid the dagger home," Walter said, waving his arms emphatically. He clutched his hands to his chest and rolled his eyes back in his head, moaning. He twirled in a circle in an exaggerated death faint before collapsing onto the kitchen table.

Darren gave him a slow clap. "You've been alone a long time, haven't you?"

Walter popped up. "I so rarely get to perform."

"While you do a lovely Lady Macbeth," I said, "Darren was poisoned, not stabbed. He never saw his attacker. No one communicated anything."

Pacing back and forth, I reviewed the facts again. "We have to be missing something."

"Maybe her son knows," Walter said.

Darren snorted. "Doubtful."

"Did she buy the poison? Seems awfully risky," I said. "Could she have used any of the plants in your garden?"

"Same problem," Walter said. "Too risky when she's paying someone else to do the deed. It would bring suspicion on her, and what if someone saw them together? The more they meet, the more likely they are to get caught."

"How can you possibly know that?"

"TV. Ghosts don't need to sleep."

A fair point. Since I was the one who started streaming old episodes of *Murder, She Wrote* to keep him from talking to me at night, I couldn't complain. At least he'd learned something useful. "Is that also where your handy knowledge of fainting symptoms comes from?"

"Nah. I got that on YouTube. Pink figured out the voice activation on the remote."

I could only think of one reason Angie would worry about Darren communicating with me after his death. "Were there any big withdrawals from your bank account recently?"

He shrugged. "I haven't noticed, but I usually only check at the end of the month. Angie handles the bill payments."

Although I didn't want to leave a trail by logging into Darren's bank accounts, I didn't know another way to get the information we needed without waiting for the bank to respond to Tim's subpoena.

When I returned to the lobby, Ben had vanished, and the TV was dark. The press conference must have ended. A glance out the window showed his car in the driveway, so I assumed he'd gone to his room. I'd have to make this quick, before he or T caught me poking around bank accounts that didn't belong to me.

First, I pulled up a private browser. Using a public

computer would have been better, but the library wouldn't be open by the time we got there.

It didn't take long to log in to Willow Falls Bank using Darren's credentials. Without him standing beside me, it would never have worked, but he easily answered the questions needed to authorize access from an unknown computer.

A list of accounts came up. Some business, some personal. Checking, savings… "What am I looking for?"

"Hold on a second." Darren leaned in, so close I'd have been able to smell his cologne if he were alive. "Pull up the joint account."

A few clicks later, a long line of transactions stared back at us. As expected, every few weeks, someone transferred funds into another Willow Falls Bank account. Clicking on the transaction showed me both Angie's and Ben's names, so Darren was right about that, at least.

Unfortunately, the transfer was smaller than Darren remembered. Fifty dollars every two weeks. I didn't know why Angie gave Ben money, but it didn't look like nearly enough to hire an assassin. The transactions started more than a year ago, but there was no way to view the total or if the money had been spent.

"You don't have Angie's password, do you?" I asked. "If her name is on Ben's account, we can check the balance and look for recent withdrawals."

"I do, but she'll get an alert that someone requested access from an unknown device. My phone probably has one, too, now that I think about it."

Trying not to let my frustration show, I returned to the activity log. Nothing unusual: the cable bill, grocery store, local pharmacy, electric bill, a payment to Chase that made my eyes pop out, a fancy high-end tea shop, Michael Kors, something that appeared to be a mortgage but looked like they'd added an extra zero.

I sighed. "I want to believe there are answers hidden here, but I'm not seeing any. There aren't any large withdrawals. Nothing conveniently going into an LLC or offshore bank account. Where did she get the money?"

The words "offshore bank account" echoed in my head.

Angie didn't have one, but Darren did. He'd said the information was on his phone—and she'd admitted going through his phone to find out if her husband was cheating.

When we spoke, Angie said she knew Darren was having an affair because she'd found an expensive gift he never gave her. She'd confronted Casey—that had to explain how they connected. If the confrontation happened around the time Casey received her diagnosis, she might have been despondent enough to agree to murder.

Darren wouldn't know any of that.

"You said the information about your hidden accounts was on your phone. What if she found out about them? Could Casey have told her?"

"They didn't know each other."

"Assume they did. Was Casey aware of the offshore accounts?"

"Only my lawyer knew. But she…" He swallowed. "Casey always picked up papers off the printer and brought them to me. She could have seen something."

"When was the last time you checked your accounts?"

If Darren hadn't been a ghost, you could've knocked him over with a feather. "You think Angie used my money to pay my killer?"

"It would explain why we're not finding any suspicious transactions here."

Navigating to another tab, I pulled up the site for

Darren's Cayman Islands bank. With his social security number and password, I logged in. The home screen listed three accounts attached to this customer, but didn't give me balances. I clicked the top link.

Darren let out a screech behind me, so loud I almost fell off my chair. "Zero balance?!"

"How much should there be?"

"A million at least, in each account. I've been saving for a while."

"Hold on. Maybe I'm looking at the wrong one." I scrolled down through the list of transactions. It didn't take long to find the information.

One week ago, someone had transferred the entire balance out of this account. The other two accounts were emptied the same day.

This couldn't be a coincidence, but I had to ask. "You didn't make those withdrawals?"

"Of course not! That was my safety net. The money was going to stay until Eve and I set up our new life."

I paused. "You said you'd never leave your wife. When I asked you about Eve at the spa, and again when Angie mentioned the prenup. You made it sound like you didn't really care about Eve."

"I was trying to protect her. If Angie killed me for cheating, who knows what she might do to my girlfriend?"

The gesture touched me. "Who would've thought Darren Cartwright was such a softie?"

"Don't you dare tell anyone."

A snort escaped me. "Your secret is safe with me. Speaking of secrets, did Eve know about these accounts?"

"Only that I was saving up for our future. Eve loves me. We wanted to be together as soon as I filed for divorce. She wouldn't have stolen from me or killed me."

I didn't think so either. Angie found these accounts. The police could verify the login IP address later, but it had to be her. She and her brother were the only people who had a claim to the money. Darren said William didn't pay attention to the finances. Casey must have told her about the secret accounts when confronted about the (non-existent) affair. Angie bided her time, made a plan. Then she withdrew the money right before he was killed so he wouldn't notice.

But how to prove my suspicions? I didn't know if the Willow Falls police could subpoena records for a bank account in the Cayman Islands, but I doubted it. Casey was being arraigned in the morning. Chief Yu was ready to close the case and take credit for solving it. She'd have Tim working on something else by lunch tomorrow.

Darren sighed. "If she hadn't suspected my assistant of dating me, none of this would have happened. What now? Do you think Detective Pratt will listen to you?"

Our theory made perfect sense to me, but still thin on physical evidence. Detective Pratt might request a search warrant, but the proof was in Darren's phone, computer, and bank accounts. If someone showed up and seized them, Angie had the resources to flee. We needed tangible proof so they could make an arrest before she realized they were on to her.

My mind raced. Between my ghost and my magic, there had to be something I could do. Josie said a truth potion would be difficult, if not impossible, but there had to be something. I needed Angie to admit what she had done.

Suddenly, it hit me. "I've got a terrible idea."

TWENTY-FOUR

Now that we knew Angie paid Casey to kill Darren, I needed to make sure she didn't get away with it. I called Tim and asked him to stop Angie from leaving the police station. That way, I could bring the printouts from Darren's bank account and confront her.

"I'd love to help, but she's gone," Tim said. "As soon as the press conference ended. Said she wanted to get to sleep early. The service is tomorrow."

"She's unfortunately not going to be able to attend," I said. "Because she'll be in jail. I'm going to get her to confess."

"Whatever you're planning, I strongly advise you to stop before I have to arrest you."

"I swear, I do not intend to do anything illegal. I am going to talk to Angie. She'll admit to paying Casey to kill her husband. If you meet me at their house, you'll be able to arrest her when she confesses."

At first, Tim argued vigorously. He didn't want me in danger. Personally, I agreed. After almost getting killed a few months ago, I'd been living happily danger-free. But considering Angie paid Casey to do the deed, she seemed unlikely to attack me personally. "Remember what Cliff said about his arrest?"

"Sometimes when I lie in bed at night, I can't think about anything else."

"I can take care of myself," I said. "Besides, you'll be outside the whole time."

Darren found the whole thing thrilling. "To think, all those years as a kid, I wanted to be a spy. Now that I'm dead, it's finally happening."

"Happy to help," I said dryly. Then into the phone, "Darren always wanted to do undercover work."

Even through the phone, I could practically hear Tim rolling his eyes. "Sure. That's what I'll tell the chief, too. I put a civilian in harm's way to help a ghost fulfill his life-long dream of being James Bond."

He continued to argue with me until I realized I could just hang up. "Listen, I'm on my way. Come or not. I'm going to get her to confess. I wish you would wire me up first, but if that's not possible, I'll call your cell when I get there. We can leave the phone line open."

"I'm not going to talk you out of this, am I?"

"Not unless you arrest me in the next fifteen minutes," I said cheerfully.

"Don't tempt me," Tim said. "I'm on my way. Do not go inside until you see me. Verify that I'm on the line before you get out of your car. If anything seems the slightest bit off, drive away."

"Deal," I lied. I refused to leave before she admitted to what she'd done. There was too much at stake. Once Angie realized we were onto her, she'd run—and with her resources, she'd never be heard from again. Those joint accounts had high balances.

It only took a minute to print the bank history showing the withdrawals. Angie would claim no knowledge of them, but I had an idea how to persuade her to tell the truth.

By the time Darren and I arrived at his house, the moon had risen high in the sky. I felt good about my plan. Was it dangerous? Yes, but I could handle myself physically. The bigger concern was that my efforts wouldn't work, and Angie would get me institutionalized.

It was a risk I would have to take. The only evidence of a payment was Casey's statement, overheard by a ghost. Her friend wouldn't be considered a credible witness. Without Angie's confession, the police chief would close the case. The press had been notified, and the killer was being arraigned tomorrow. Angie would get away with paying someone to kill her husband.

Darren went in first to confirm she was alone in the house. I didn't want to give Ben's nana a heart attack. A minute later, Darren gave me the go ahead. While he was inside, Tim parked in front of the house next door.

Once I set up an open phone line so he could hear what happened, it was show time.

"Here goes nothing." Taking a deep breath, I threw my shoulders back and walked to the front porch with confidence.

When Angie opened the door, she looked baffled. "What are you doing here?"

"Can I come in? I'd like to talk about your husband."

"No. I'm sorry, I don't think so. Darren is gone. The police caught the woman who killed him, and I'd like to be alone in my grief."

"Yes, I heard that, too. But we know it's not the full story, don't we?"

She tried to close the door in my face. It had been a long couple of days, and I wasn't terribly interested in niceties. A blast of magic shot through the door, grabbing her pants and dragging them into the center of the room. Angie shrieked and released her grip on the knob. "What is happening? What are you doing to me?"

Ignoring her questions, I shut the door. "Thank you for inviting me in. You have such a lovely home."

"My son is upstairs. If you don't leave now, I'll have him remove you."

"Ben is at my bed-and-breakfast. He rented a room to avoid you." A half-truth, but I wanted to keep her off guard. "And I know your mother isn't here, either."

Fear entered her eyes. "I don't know what you're doing here, but I'm going to call the police."

"Excellent plan! Let's tell them how you killed your husband."

She sputtered. I let her go for a minute, then said, "Should we chat in the living room?"

Angie found her composure so quickly it was impressive. Head high, she led me into the living room. After leading me to a chair, she paused in front of the sofa. "Would you like a cup of tea? I could step into the kitchen and be back before you know it."

"No, thank you." I smiled sweetly. "I don't think you should go anywhere until we've discussed this. Darren is here with me. He knows you hired Casey to kill him, and he has a few questions."

"Here. With you?"

"Yes. Since I was in the spa when you had him killed, his ghost seemed to have latched onto me."

"Ghost? Oh, dear!" Her eyes rolled up into her head, and she flopped backward onto the couch. Exactly like the first time. An odd reaction from someone who claimed to believe in spirits and engaged a psychic. Now I recognized it as an avoidance tactic.

"I know you didn't faint. I'm not leaving until you talk to me."

She maintained the act for forty-five seconds before apparently deciding it would be better to go on the offensive. She sat, smoothing her hair before glaring at me. "This is absurd. Ghosts aren't real, and you are trespassing. I'm calling the police."

"Great. They would love to hear your confession."

Instead of answering, she rose to her feet. I sent a burst of magic into her wool pants. Sheep were herd animals, happy to follow the leader. Once I convinced one section of fabric to cling to the couch, the rest followed. The threads holding her seams together released themselves. Angie froze when the fabric fluttered. Then I made it billow.

She screamed, "What are you doing? Stop this instant!"

"Oh, don't worry about me." I sent another request, and the threads wove themselves into the couch, forcing Angie to take a hard seat. "Why did you do it?"

"I'm not saying a word. You're not talking to my husband."

"I am, and I can prove it. Ask me anything."

"Ask him when my birthday is."

"June 9," Darren said promptly. I repeated it.

Angie snorted. "I should have asked something he actually knew. What's my favorite color?"

"She loves yellow, because it's so happy, but she thinks people will think she's too brash if she says it. She claims it's navy blue," Darren said. "That necklace she's hiding is a sunflower."

Around Angie's neck, I spotted a gold chain peeking out of the collar of her shirt. I gestured toward it. "Darren says you're wearing a sunflower because you love yellow, but you tell everyone your favorite color is navy."

Instantly, her face changed. "You really are talking to him!"

"I am."

"Then he can tell you I wasn't at the spa when he died. I've never been there. I was at the zoo. Ask anyone who was at the fundraiser. I didn't do anything, and you can't prove I did. The police caught the killer. She confessed. If you leave now, I won't have you arrested for kidnapping."

"You made a mistake telling me you'd gone to confront Casey about her relationship with Darren. Shortly before that, she got arrested for getting drunk in public. Her scene made perfect sense once I discovered she'd found out she only had a few months to live."

"It's terribly sad," Angie said. "But I don't understand what that has to do with me."

"When Casey found out about her diagnosis, she was devastated. She didn't know who would pay for her mother's care. You came up with a plan."

"You should write mystery novels. You're better than Sue Grafton." Angie tried to kick me, but the threads—and my magic—held fast. A scream of frustration escaped before she slipped her mask of composure back into place. "I've hit the emergency panic button. The police will be here momentarily."

Darren snorted. "We don't have a panic button."

I repeated what he said, and her eyes widened. "You're serious."

"If you didn't believe me, why did you pretend to faint —twice?"

"Twice?"

Too late, I remembered she had no recollection of my first visit. "You didn't want him to tell me you killed him. Or, if I already knew, you wanted to distract me. Guess what? We figured it out."

"You realize you sound crazy, right? Especially since you're holding me hostage."

"If I were in your position, I would worry about myself," I said. "You were devastated when you found out your husband was seeing a younger woman. I don't blame you. I'm a little surprised you went after him and not her."

"If that's true, why wouldn't I divorce him? You forget I've got a prenup."

I pulled out the printed bank activity and handed it to her. "Because he's been embezzling from your brother. You get a divorce, he takes the money and runs. If he dies, it all comes back to you."

"This isn't my account."

"No, it's not. That's the brilliance of the scheme. Using your husband's own embezzled funds to kill him was inspired. If anyone dug into those accounts, you could swear you knew nothing about them."

"You think you're so smart, don't you?"

"Not really. Your husband told me everything."

"Of course he did. You know what? Tell the police. No one will believe you." She laughed, a sound close enough to a cackle to make the hair on my neck stand up. "My husband's ghost told you I killed him. It's absurd! You can't take the stand. My lawyer would crucify you. I've got no record. I'm a pillar of the community. All you have is a dying woman who confessed to murder and bank accounts belonging to someone else."

"Maybe you're right. Or maybe I have a ghost who has sworn to haunt you until you admit to killing him."

She didn't know her husband's spirit couldn't hurt her. But she knew weird things started when I arrived.

I hesitated, just for a heartbeat. If this failed like the memory spell, Darren's killer would get away unscathed. But that was a new spell. This used ambient magic, which ran through my veins. I could do this.

My power flowed through the house, searching for several articles of clothing pressed together: a closet. Hopefully Angie hadn't packed up her husband's things yet. I could do this with her clothes, but his would carry a greater impact.

The fabrics on the left side of the closet were cold, alone. Like they didn't belong. When I asked for help, they eagerly hopped to life.

Something clattered above us. A dozen wooden hangers hit the floor as the garments pulled themselves off the rack.

"What's that?" Angie asked, glancing at the ceiling.

"I tried to reason with you," I said. "Darren knows you killed him. He can't move on until you admit it. If you don't apologize, he'll stay. But he wants to give you a chance to rethink things."

A thick silence filled the air. I let Angie consider my words while calling each expensive Italian suit down the stairs, marching toward me as if the fabric had developed free will.

The pant legs alternated steps in perfect unison; the right and left sleeves swung together.

Her eyes widened when she saw the first suit. They kept coming. Angie trembled, and I almost felt bad for her.

Almost. She remained silent, so I asked the suits to line up in a half circle facing the couch. When one sleeve lifted itself toward her face to stroke her cheek, Angie screamed.

"Okay, fine! I did it! But you deserved it, you cheating jerk!"

The suits paused mid-air. "Did what?"

"Oh, you know what," she snapped. "I paid Casey to kill Darren. It was bad enough that he was cheating on me. But then I found out he'd been *stealing* from my family. Oh, no. That wasn't going to happen."

As one, the suits dropped to a heap at her feet.

"Hey! Watch the Italian silk," Darren protested.

"Thank you for your confession. Don't you feel better?"

Angie shot daggers at me with her eyes. "Hardly. After all Darren put me through, he doesn't get to haunt me for eternity. I've suffered enough. Now you got what you wanted, go away."

"You didn't apologize."

"And I'm not going to. Let me up and leave my home."

"The police are on their way."

She snorted. "They'll never believe you."

"Don't be so sure. Your confession rang pretty true."

"I wanted to make it look like a suicide, keep it clean. No investigation, no autopsy, and we all move on. Unfortunately, the only thing Darren loved more than money was himself. No one would have believed he'd lost the will to live."

"Ouch," Darren said. "You want to know what people think of you, come back as a ghost."

"Well, she's right about one thing. You loved life. You weren't ready for it to end."

"Yeah." He sighed heavily. "Being dead is the pits."

Angie looked at me and scowled. "I would have gotten

away with it, too. No one should have made the connection. Too bad Casey ran her big mouth."

"She never said a word." Well, not to me, anyway.

"Then how did you figure it out?"

I smiled sweetly. "A magician never reveals her secrets."

Three loud knocks at the door signaled we'd gotten what we needed. Opening it, I found Tim. Angie swore when he followed me into the living room. She struggled to stand, but the threads woven into the couch held.

Tim gaped for a long moment, unable to maintain his composure. Angie insisted he let her up immediately. He just kept staring.

Finally, he turned to me. "This looks like something I don't want to ask too many questions about."

"She's a witch!" Angie yelled. "She put a spell on me."

"You don't say?" Tim deserved an Oscar for this performance. Even with his daughter's psychic friend, he was taking things remarkably well. "I thought you sewed yourself into your couch. Emma, did you do this?"

Putting on my most innocent look, I said, "I have no idea what you're talking about." With a silent wave of my fingers, I returned Angie's clothes to normal. Tim recited her Miranda rights. The couch repaired itself. Everything looked like I'd never touched it.

Tim looked from the couch to me, then back as he helped Angie to her feet and cuffed her. Eventually, he just shook his head. He must have realized there was no reasonable explanation.

Darren and I watched Tim take Angie to the waiting patrol car. Then a thought occurred to me.

"Hey, Tim?"

"Yeah?"

"What's going to happen to Casey?"

"She gave a full confession, Emma. She knew things only the killer could know."

"But she was desperate!"

"A lot of desperate people don't resort to murder."

I sighed. "You're right."

"If she's willing to testify against Angie, she might get some consideration."

"What about the money?"

He shook his head. "It's evidence."

Even knowing he was right, my heart hurt at the idea of Casey's sacrifice being for nothing. Her mother would be alone, and when the money ran out, she'd be moved to a state-run facility.

Unless I stepped in.

Tim slammed the door shut, cutting off Angie's tirade. "Never, ever tell me what happened in there."

"My lips are sealed." I smiled sweetly at him. "That was fun. Thanks."

"Remind me not to cross you." He walked around the car and got into the driver's seat.

Watching his wife in the backseat, Darren sighed. "Such a spitfire. I've missed that."

"You missed the anger that led to her killing you?"

"No, the passion. Angie was so *alive* when we met, full of fire. Interested in helping people. She wanted to change the world. Then, somehow, she decided the way to do that was to host charity luncheons. I never would have strayed if she hadn't changed."

"You know that doesn't make it okay, right?" I said.

"I know you judge me." He glanced around and sighed. "What now?"

We watched Detective Pratt start the police car and drive down the street.

"Now, we wait for trial, I guess. Do you want to go?"

"Nah." He thought for a bit, then said, "I think I'm good. I feel peaceful. There's nothing left for me here."

An ornate door shimmered into view. Martha's entry to the afterlife had been plain and serviceable, just like her. This double door stood fifteen feet high, with massive windows in each and an arch at the top. A gold design etched into the glass created a D on one door, a C on the other.

Darren looked at it, then me, then whistled. "You see that?"

I nodded.

"Guess this is it," he said.

"It is. You've worked hard all your life. It's time to enjoy your death."

He snorted. "If they want me to enjoy it, I hope they've got clients to woo in there. I loved my job."

The door opened. On the other side, a bustling bar scene waited. Women danced on a stage, a buzz of conversation, and loud laughter.

"Now that's what I'm talking about," Darren said as he floated toward the entrance. "Thanks for the help."

As he stepped across the threshold, the door closed behind him, cutting off all sounds within.

The door and light faded.

EPILOGUE

After Darren went through his door, the drive back to the mansion felt oddly lonely. This was the first time I'd been in my new Porsche without him. Darren was an acquired taste, but I'd gotten used to having him around.

The deafening silence made me realize how much I missed Walter. As confusing as it had been to have two ghosts bickering, I'd barely seen him the past few days. His presence usually reassured me. I hoped he wouldn't be upset at our separation, but there hadn't been a choice: Darren needed me. Walter was the one who told me to use my powers for good. And he didn't want to be around Darren more than necessary.

When I reached the top of my driveway, my grandfather was waiting on the front porch. I didn't waste any time getting out of the car to greet him.

"Where's your friend?" he asked.

"He found his door," I said. "With a little persuading, Angie confessed. It was great. You should have come."

Walter snorted. "I got more than enough of that guy.

What an oaf. Unbearable in life, just as bad in death. Me being around wouldn't have helped if I was constantly telling him to shut his trap."

"You're right." I met his eyes and smiled. "Thanks for your help earlier. If I could give you a hug, I absolutely would."

He bumped his hip up to mine. "So you saved the day. What's next?"

"Well, we missed our day of R&R. Do you want to go skydiving?"

His laugh rang out. "We've had enough excitement. Maybe next week. You need a break."

"I'm so glad you said that."

Inside, I queued up Walter's favorite old baseball reruns on ESPN and went to tell Josie the mystery had been solved. She and T waited for me in the kitchen.

"Are you still going to the police station with me?" T asked.

In all the excitement, I'd completely forgotten. The second time this week I'd bailed on this poor kid. At this rate, he'd never trust me. I took a deep breath. "Absolutely. We'll go in a couple of days. Detective Pratt is going to be pretty busy the rest of the night. I was hoping tomorrow you could teach me how to tell which plants are weeds. I hear gardening is good for the soul."

"You got it."

"While we're out there, you can tell me what really happened with your parents."

BEING in the garden and sunshine must have made talking easier. While we worked, T told me that his parents told him to leave after he came out to them.

"Maybe they miss you. Would you be willing to talk to them if they apologize?"

He shrugged. "Talk, maybe. I don't want to go back. I never felt like they liked me for who I was."

My heart broke for him.

After lunch, I took a batch of Josie's special cookies and went to have a talk with his parents. They eventually agreed to drop the missing persons inquiry if T called so they could talk. It would be a long road toward repairing their relationship, but T seemed happy they'd taken the first step. Meanwhile, he'd stay in the mansion, tending the gardens. He had my old car if he wanted to visit them.

When I got home, I settled behind my desk to catch up on the mail that had arrived in the past few days. After about an hour, footsteps on the stairs reminded me that Ben was still staying in one of my rooms. If I were running this place for profit, I would be the worst B&B owner ever. No advertising, no income, forgets about her guests. Good thing the rooms were self-cleaning.

"This one's cute," Walter said. "A little young, but he's not a killer. Big step up from the last guy."

It was getting easier to keep my eyes on my guest. "Good morning. How are you? I'm sorry to hear about your mom."

"Thanks." Ben sighed. "I can't believe she killed him. I mean, I hated the guy, but still."

"Love can drive people to do things you'd never expect," I said. "Especially when you combine love and money. She must have been furious to learn he was stealing from your family."

"Yeah. I get it. They used to fight a lot. A week ago, I'd have said she was better off without him. But I never thought she had it in her. It'll take me some time to wrap my head around everything."

"Are you moving back to the house?"

"I'd been thinking of staying in the area for a bit, but no. I can't stand the thought of living in that house now. Nana went home this morning. I'd be completely alone."

"I understand. You're welcome here as long as you want." Time to navigate toward less emotionally charged waters. "How's the room?"

"It's great. But listen, I came down to ask for a personal favor."

"What's up?"

"There are some people in town, saying some stuff about you." His face was so red I decided to make this easier on him.

"I'm not surprised to hear that. Last month, someone accused me of murder." I shook my head ruefully. "What's the big rumor now?"

"You seemed skeptical about Mom having a psychic, but the more I thought about it, it didn't fit. Especially after I thought about the things people have been saying. It's going to sound pretty out there."

"More out there than people saying I killed my breakfast chef on the day she started?"

"No." He relaxed a fraction. "I feel stupid saying this. But I've been wanting to buy a bar for a long time, and now I'm going to get Darren's life insurance money. Apparently, my mom can't inherit on account of killing him."

"Let me stop you," I said. "If there are any rumors that I could be remotely useful at operating a bar or serving drinks, you've been sadly misinformed."

"No, it's not that." He shifted a bit, smoothed his hair, then raised his head to meet my gaze as if making a decision. "It's the bar we talked about before. The one in Shady Grove."

"Ah." Everything fell into place.

"Exactly." Ben cleared his throat. "The town foreclosed the property a while back for unpaid property taxes. If I pay the debt, it's mine. But rumor says it's haunted. The woman at the magic shop said you might help. I don't believe in ghosts or anything... Or at least, I don't think I do. But the place has a weird history. I'm lost. Can you help me?"

I smiled. "I'll see what I can do."

Is the Shady Grove Bar haunted? Is it cursed? Can Emma help Ben reopen it after all these years? Find out in Book 3: OPEN FOR WITCHNESS.

GET A FREE NOVELLA!

After a busy winter of murder-solving, Aly can't wait to relax with some family fun at the Shady Grove Annual Treasure Hunt. For twenty-five years, town residents have searched futilely for a chest containing the deed to an abandoned mansion on the edge of town. At this point, Aly's pretty sure the treasure is a myth, but she's always up for Shady Grove shenanigans.

When the Treasure Hunt gets underway, a suspicious new resident throws everything into question. Someone's got a hidden motive for participating, and the town may be in danger. Can Aly solve the mystery to save the day?

MYSTIC TREASURE PREVIEW

Today was the perfect day to win a fortune. I wasn't the only one who thought so: The Shady Grove Town Square hummed with excitement. Fluffy white cumulus clouds peppered the sky. Between the slight breeze and the mercury topping out at seventy degrees, this was the kind of gorgeous summer day that made it worth living through the humidity and thundershowers.

Half the town must have turned out to watch this event. Granted, half the town meant a few thousand people, but still. Town Square was bursting at the seams. Set near the end of Main Street, the largest park in town ran a block down to Second Street, with the other end across the street from City Hall. My three-year-old nephew and I stood under a tree, soaking it all in while we waited for my brother to join us.

Thankfully, Kyle hadn't yet seen the guy making balloon animals. On the corner nearest me, a marching band warmed up their instruments, complete with a bagpipes player. Town residents milled around, visiting the booths that had been set up to feed and entertain us. A huge banner extended across the square, welcoming everyone to the "WALTER SPARROW ANNUAL MEMORIAL TREASURE HUNT".

According to the rumor mill, Walter Sparrow was some eccentric millionaire who died about twenty-five years ago. Instead of leaving his money to a relative or a friend or a local animal shelter, he created this big annual party for everyone to try to win the big prize. No one had managed yet. My best friend Rusty suspected the entire story was a lie, and Walter just wanted to make sure we all talked about him forever after he passed.

Considering the amount of money supposedly on the line, I was surprised there weren't fortune hunters sniffing around all year, but Shady Grove wasn't like other towns. Maybe the same forces that led to unusual happenings kept outsiders away?

Or maybe our town was so tiny that no one outside a fifty-mile radius had heard of Shady Grove or old Walter? That was more likely.

Personally, I suspected Rusty was right. The whole thing sounded like an urban legend. An excuse for a big summer party, but anyone expecting to find treasure would be sorely disappointed. Still, we'd teamed up and gotten ready for action. The practice solving clues should come in handy once Rusty finished getting his PI license.

Tugging my hand, Kyle peered up at me with his big brown eyes and heart-shaped face from beneath his adorably oversized sun hat. "What's a treasure hunt, Aunt Aly?"

I resisted smoothing an errant chestnut curl that was so like mine. "It means Rusty and I are going to follow clues to find a lost item that has been hidden somewhere in the town."

"I find it! What did Rusty lose?" Kyle asked.

I grinned at the spark of excitement in his eyes and smoothed a curl off of his forehead. My nephew had been born with the power to find lost objects, a secret we preferred to keep from the rest of the world as long as possible. Psychic powers ran in our family, but we'd recently learned that some people wanted to exploit what he could do. "Thanks, Little Man, but this game is for adults only. Besides, in a game, it's not fair to use our special abilities to win."

"Cheating?"

"Yes, that's considered cheating."

"Oh. I won't cheat." Kyle stuck out his lower lip. Then his gaze landed on one of the tables below the "WALTER SPARROW MEMORIAL TREASURE HUNT" banner. "Cookie?"

With a laugh, I let him drag me to the table, manned by my friend and the owner of the local coffee shop, Julie Capaldi. A self-described "recovering lawyer," Julie was a blue-eyed blonde who'd moved to Shady Grove a few years ago to take over her aunt's business. She'd set out cookies for sale, but also—and more importantly—iced coffee.

"Hey! Looking forward to the hunt?" she asked when we got within earshot.

"You know it," I said. "Rusty's excited to practice his PI skills. I'm here to stop him from picking the locks of every store on Main Street."

She laughed. "He's going to be a great investigator. I miss having him at the cafe, though."

Until recently, Rusty had worked as the manager at On What Grounds?. After helping me learn to use my powers and solve a murder, my new best friend discovered his true calling. I often considered myself fortunate Julie hadn't banned me from her store when he left. Where would I get my coffee?

Then again, I suspected she had a thing for my brother.

"Hey, kiddo!" she said to Kyle before offering him a cookie. "You planning to hunt treasure today?"

"Aunt Aly said I was cheating."

My face flamed. Maybe she wouldn't understand him? Three-year-olds didn't have the best enunciation, and his mouth was full of cookie. I wasn't sure how much Julie knew, either about Kyle's abilities or mine. She certainly hadn't heard it from me, but small towns didn't have many secrets.

"Cheating? That's no good." She gave me one of those 'kids say the darnedest things' grins.

In response, I gave her the most innocent look I could muster. "We're learning new words this week. Anyway, are you entering?"

"No, I can't."

"Can't?"

She shook her head and laughed. "I did it last year. You're only allowed to enter once."

"That's odd," I said. "Kevin did it last year, too. I thought he wasn't entering because he wanted to spend the day with Kyle."

"That's part of it, I'm sure. But yeah, everyone gets one chance." She shrugged. "People with money are eccentric, right? It's Walter's estate, so he gets to make the rules. I'll send all my good vibes to you and Rusty."

At the mention of my partner, I turned to scan the crowd. With the pre-hunt festivities drawing to an end, Town Square had cleared out somewhat. A lot of people still stood around, but most moved to ring the center, where the hunt would soon begin.

About fifteen feet away, I spotted my friend Tiffaneigh Pratt talking to Brad Stevens. The three of us studied science together at Maloney College. She still didn't want to admit they were dating, but the two of them looked awfully cozy. Their matching bright blue shirts with "WALTER SPARROW HUNTER" on the back told me everything I needed to know about their relationship—and my primary competition. Tiffaneigh hated to lose, and she had some flexible ideas about what constituted fair and legal gameplay.

We'd need to keep an eye on her if we wanted to win.

Mystic Treasure is ONLY available by signing up for my newsletter - visit www.adabell.com to get your copy.

ACKNOWLEDGMENTS

Several months ago, while enjoying a day of relaxation to celebrate my friend's birthday, I said casually, "If you wanted to kill someone at a day spa, how would you do it?"

To her credit, my friend neither screamed nor called the police on me. Instead, she instantly said she'd slip poison in their drink. The room where people waited for their services was so dark, she said, no one would notice, and everyone would assume he was sleeping until the spa closed for the night.

Thank you, Deana, for being unflappable, insightful, and every bit as weird as me. Your plan worked out much better than my initial idea of having Darren smothered while on the massage table.

Huge thanks to my fellow Scofflaws for entertaining me endlessly with suggestions of ear worms that would make you immediately do someone's bidding, if only to get them to stop singing. I wound up with dozens of excellent options, but hopefully no one else will try Darren's tactics to get Emma's help.

Again, thank you to all of my Kickstarter backers, but especially to those who exhibited enormous faith in me by purchasing the entire catalog: GhostCat, Kris D'Anci, Michelle and John Redding, Sharon Friedman, Stephanie Thornton, Aylkaraemi, Dana, Erin Ratelle, Wendy Altenhof, Hana Correa, Heidi Kruger, Jamie Dill, Jenn Morris, John

Idlor, Kimberly Lloyd, Koni Foster, Lauren Hall, Lynne Freeman, Melody Smith, Michelle L., Myrrdin Starfari, Oliver Gross, Rhel ná DecVandé, Rhonda Peek, Robert Anthony Pritchard, and Stormi Lewis.

HAUNTED HAVEN
SERIES

Emma thought life was weird before she found out she was a witch. Now she's got some pretty cool powers, a snarky-yet-insightful talking cat, and a fabulous mansion-turned-B&B, complete with ghost. Here is your complete guide to the *Haunted Haven* series.

Unfinished Witchness: Emma is thrilled to come into her legacy: not only has she inherited stacks of money and a mansion, she's got magic! Everything is coming up roses until she finds her new chef dead in the kitchen and her other employee accused of murder. If she can't find the real killer, this haunted haven might never open for business.

Risky Witchness: Now that Emma's bed and breakfast is bustling with activity, she decides to treat herself to some R&R at the local fancy spa. But when she finds another guest dead, Emma becomes the prime suspect. She'll need the help of his ghost to help find the real killer before they find her.

OPEN FOR WITCHNESS: When Ben convinces Emma to investigate the mysteriously closed bar in Shady Grove, she discovers it's being guarded by an extremely unpleasant spirit. The only way to help her friend is to solve the mystery—but the trail has been cold for decades. Can she close the case and reopen the bar?

A SHADY GROVE CHRONOLOGY

Ever since twenty-one-year-old Aluminum Reynolds moved to Shady Grove, New York, her life has been full of surprises. Here's a list of Aly's adventures, in chronological order.

MYSTIC PIECES: Aly doesn't believe in psychics. Too bad she just had her first vision. Her first instinct is flat-out denial. After all, science and magic don't mix. But when a man is murdered, Aly realizes that she may be able to use her strange new "gifts" to find the culprit. If she can avoid getting herself killed in the process.

THE SCRY'S THE LIMIT: Aly's just starting to get the hang of her psychic gifts when she literally stumbles over her favorite professor's body. She's devastated and determined to get justice. But with several people benefitting from Professor Zimm's death, how will Aly find the real culprit before they find her?

. . .

SIGHT SEERING: As a psychic who gains powers from antiques, Aly is ecstatic to be invited to an estate sale. It's only after she arrives that she discovers the estate's owner didn't die in her sleep—she was murdered.

MYSTIC TREASURE: Aly and Rusty are excited to participate in the annual Walter Sparrow Treasure Hunt. As the event gets underway, they realize that there's more to this event than meets the eye. Someone's got a hidden motive for participating, and the entire town may be in danger.

THIS NOVELLA TAKES place between the final chapters and epilogue of *Sight Seering*. *Mystic Treasure* is ONLY available by signing up for my newsletter at www.adabell.com. Thank you for hanging out with me!

SEER TODAY, Gone Tomorrow: Just when Aly finally identified her sister-in-law's killer, they got away—and they're not alone. To make matters worse, someone powerful has cursed the residents of Shady Grove. Aly's powers vanish. Without her psychic gifts, how will Aly find Katrina's killer and save the pet store?

THE PIE IN THE SCRY: After nearly a year, Aly's got a plan to bring Katrina's killer to justice. But before she and Kevin can implement it, she has a vision of someone murdering

Tony, the bakery owner. As if that wasn't bad enough—the killer looks exactly like Aly.

<u>Mystic Persons</u>: Aly just completed the biggest spell she's ever attempted, with a little help. But the magic came with an unexpected side effect, and now she's got to figure out what happened to the dead man in the upstairs bath before her parents arrive for the holidays.

WRITTEN AS LAURA HEFFERNAN

Retail to Riches Series

A Royal Farce: After years of secretly crushing on her friend Pierre, Lila is thrilled when he proposes they start a fake relationship. For weeks, she finds herself hoping their farce could turn into the real thing—but Pierre's hiding a secret of royal magnitude.

A Royal Pain: When Lila and Pierre arrive in Corchenne to meet her in-laws, she's shocked to discover that her scheming brother has already arrived. Can their marriage survive Caleb's shenanigans and the weight of royal expectations?

The Reality Star Series

America's Next Reality Star: Jen went on a reality show to compete for the $250,000 grand prize. But when she finds herself battling another woman for co-competitor Justin's heart, she finds herself wondering what the true prize is.

Sweet Reality: After a killer competitor threatens her new business, Jen sets sail on a new reality show adventure to save the day. But Ariana's back, and she's determined to end Jen and Justin's relationship once and for all.

Reality Wedding: After retiring from reality TV, Jen receives an offer she can't refuse. The Network wants Jen and Justin to film their wedding to fill an empty time slot—and if they refuse, the Network will get Justin fired.

The Gamer Girls Series

She's Got Game: Gwen's dedicated to becoming the American Board Games Champion, and she never ever mixes gaming with pleasure. But when she meets Cody, trying to resist his charm becomes a losing proposition.

Against the Rules: For years, Holly has harbored a secret crush on her best friend's dad. Nathan is young, he's hot. What's a little harmless flirtation while playing games? But when she discovers that Nathan returns her feelings, Holly may have to choose between two of the most important people in her life.

Make Your Move: Shannon's more interested in designing games and rising to the top at work than dating. She's surprised to find herself falling for her roommate, Tyler. Worse, he's dating her boss's daughter. If she makes her move, Shannon could get fired.

Push and Pole Series

Poll Dancer: A delightfully modern twist on *My Fair Lady*: When a promotional video for her pole-dancing classes goes viral, Mel comes under fire from a local politician running for senate. Desperate to save her studio, Mel decides her only option is to launch her own campaign — and win!

The Accidental Senator: After accidentally finding herself elected state senator, Lana Chen is determined to prove her worth. But when a mistake aids the passage of a bill that's going to put her best friend out of business, Lana has to set things right before it's too late.

Standalone Books

Finding Tranquility: Christa Cooper finds the courage to transition after she nearly loses her life on September 11. Eighteen years later, she's confronted by the wife she left behind: Jess, who discovers that the person she knew as Brett is now Christa. Can they find a future together, despite the past?

Anna's Guide to Getting Even: Anna's perfect life has turned into a string of disasters: After a hurricane destroys her house, her ex publicizes private photos of her — which costs Anna her job and her current boyfriend. And after hitting rock bottom, she decides that revenge is the only way forward...

Friction: Britt's always avoided relationships. Then, weeks before she's set to move away, she meets Colin. To her surprise, she finds herself wanting more.